Acting Edition

Ken Ludwig's
The Three
Musketeers

Adapted from the novel by
Alexandre Dumas

Lit. A
Michael W.

FOR PRODUCTION INQUIRIES

UNITED STATES AND CANADA
info@concordtheatricals.com
1-866-979-0447

UNITED KINGDOM AND EUROPE
licensing@concordtheatricals.co.uk
020-7054-7298

Each title is subject to availability from Concord Theatricals Corp., depending upon country of performance. Please be aware that THE THREE MUSKETEERS may not be licensed by Concord Theatricals Corp. in your territory. Professional and amateur producers should contact the nearest Concord Theatricals Corp. office or licensing partner to verify availability.

No one shall make any changes in this title(s) for the purpose of production. No part of this book may be reproduced, stored in a retrieval system, scanned, uploaded, or transmitted in any form, by any means, now known or yet to be invented, including mechanical, electronic, digital, photocopying, recording, videotaping, or otherwise, without the prior written permission of the publisher. No one shall share this title(s), or any part of this title(s), through any social media or file hosting websites.

For all inquiries regarding motion picture, television, online/digital and other media rights, please contact Concord Theatricals Corp.

MUSIC AND THIRD-PARTY MATERIALS USE NOTE

Licensees are solely responsible for obtaining formal written permission from copyright owners to use copyrighted music and/or other copyrighted third-party materials (e.g., artworks, logos) in the performance of this play and are strongly cautioned to do so. If no such permission is obtained by the licensee, then the licensee must use only original music and materials that the licensee owns and controls. Licensees are solely responsible and liable for clearances of all third-party copyrighted materials, including without limitation music, and shall indemnify the copyright owners of the play(s) and their licensing agent, Concord Theatricals Corp., against any costs, expenses, losses and liabilities arising from the use of such copyrighted third-party materials by licensees. For music, please contact the appropriate music licensing authority in your territory for the rights to any incidental music.

IMPORTANT BILLING AND CREDIT REQUIREMENTS

If you have obtained performance rights to this title, please refer to your licensing agreement for important billing and credit requirements.

THE THREE MUSKETEERS had its world premiere on December 6, 2006 in the United Kingdom at the world-famous Bristol Old Vic. The production was under the direction of Tim Sheader, assisted by Beckie Mills. The fight director was Richard Ryan, with music by Corin Buckeridge, design by Laura Hopkins, sound by Jason Barnes, lighting by Bruno Poet, and choreography by Frances Newman. The artistic director of the theater was Simon Reade. The stage manager was Claire Yapp, with deputy stage manager Linda Muirhead assisted by Laura Levis and Michelle Keeling. The cast was as follows:

D'ARTAGNAN . . . . George Rainsford
SABINE . . . . Samantha Robinson
CARDINAL RICHELIEU . . . . Robin Sebastian
PORTHOS . . . . Paul Agar
ARAMIS . . . . Vyelle Croom
ATHOS . . . . Gerald Kyd
ROCHEFORT . . . . Paul Benzing
MILADY . . . . Laura Rogers
TREVILLE . . . . Marcello Walton
CONSTANCE . . . . Charity Wakefield
KING LOUIS . . . . Julien Ball
QUEEN ANNE . . . . Fiona Dunn

This new edition of Ken Ludwig's *THE THREE MUSKETEERS* replaces the older edition and was first produced at Pennsylvania Shakespeare Festival (Patrick Mulcahy, Producing Artistic Director; Casey William Gallagher, Managing Director) on July 14, 2017. The production was under the direction of Rick Sordelet. The fight director was Christian Kelly-Sordelet, with music and sound by Alexander Sovronsky, costume design by Samantha Fleming, lighting by Masha Tsimring, and scenic design by Brian Sidney Bembridge. The stage manager was Alison Hassman*, assisted by Carolyn Reich*. The cast was as follows:

D'ARTAGNAN	Sean Patrick Higgins*
SABINE	Stephanie Hodge
CARDINAL RICHELIEU	Paul Kiernan*
PORTHOS	Zack Robidas*
ARAMIS	Alexander Sovronsky*
ATHOS	Ian Merrill Peakes*
ROCHEFORT	John Keabler*
MILADY	Stella Baker
TREVILLE	Esau Pritchett*
CONSTANCE	Kelsey Rainwater
KING LOUIS	Dan Hodge*
QUEEN ANNE	Marnie Schulenburg*
BUCKINGHAM	Mike Rossmy*
STANLEY	John Keabler*
OLD LADY	Stella Baker
ENSEMBLE	Michael Covel, Austin Lucas, Dane McMichael, Ilia Paulino, Andrew T. Scoggin, Victoria Scovens

*Member of Actors' Equity Association, the Union of Professional Stage Actors, or Stage Managers in the United States.

CHARACTERS

MEN (eight with doubling)

D'ARTAGNAN

ATHOS

PORTHOS

ARAMIS

CARDINAL RICHELIEU

ROCHEFORT / STANLEY

KING LOUIS / D'ARTAGNAN'S FATHER / BASILLE / FOUQUET / FACHE

TREVILLE / DUKE OF BUCKINGHAM / RAVANCHE / RUFFIAN / INKEEPER / DEBRIS

WOMEN (four with doubling)

SABINE

MILADY / OLD WOMAN

CONSTANCE BONACIEUX / ADELE / SISTER

QUEEN ANNE / D'ARTAGNAN'S MOTHER / ELISE / MOTHER SUPERIOR / ABBESS

For my dad,
the best of all fathers,

and

to Jim Davidson,
inestimable friend and fellow writer,
who has suffered through many a plot discussion
and has lived to tell about it

ACT I

Scene One

(The play begins when three sword fighters burst into view. They fight in earnest, coming perilously close to maiming each other for life.)

(We are outside a farmhouse in Gascony in the spring of 1625. One of the fighters is a man in his fifties. The other two fighters are younger, the boy in his early twenties, the girl about seventeen. All are simply dressed as yeomen. First one has the advantage, then the other. They really go at it hammer and tongs; grunting, shouting, and crying out, each trying desperately to kill the other with all his or her might. At last, the older man gets the advantage and, using a special sword trick – "Hey! Snap! Ha!" – disarms the two young fighters and holds the point of his sword at the young man's throat. The young man quails for a moment, then breaks into a smile.)

*(The young man's name is **D'ARTAGNAN**. He is Youth. He is Courage. He is Hope. The young woman's name is **SABINE**, and she is full of wonder and mischief, ready to take on the world. The older man is their **FATHER**.)*

D'ARTAGNAN. Father, how do you do that?!

SABINE. It's like a magic trick.

FATHER. Misdirection. Get your opponent to lose his focus, then move like lightning. Hey! Snap! Ha!

(He's done it again.)

If you want to conquer worlds, concentrate. Draw your mind to the center, like a magnet. Couple that with common sense, a will to succeed, a kind heart, and you will move mountains.

D'ARTAGNAN. Like our father.

FATHER. *(To* **SABINE**.*)* Now off with you, I must speak to my son.

*(***SABINE** *exits.)*

It's time you were going.

D'ARTAGNAN. Did you leave home at my age, sir?

FATHER. Yes, and for the same reason. To be a musketeer.

D'ARTAGNAN. I dream about it every night. Fighting duels, defending the king, standing up to the cardinal and his –

FATHER. Stop.

D'ARTAGNAN. What?

FATHER. Never say that. You do not want Cardinal Richelieu as your enemy.

D'ARTAGNAN. But he opposes the king at every turn. They say he has spies everywhere.

FATHER. Just stay away from him. If, by the grace of God, you become a musketeer some day, your job is to defend the king and protect the queen.

D'ARTAGNAN. But the cardinal is their enemy.

FATHER. Not openly. He wouldn't dare. Just do your duty and never engage the cardinal directly. Is that clear?

D'ARTAGNAN. Yes, sir.

(Grumbles.) Unless he starts it first...

FATHER. Here. Take my sword. You'll need it.

D'ARTAGNAN. *(Overwhelmed.)* Father...

FATHER. Use it well, to fight for justice. For justice, like mercy, is divine and deserves your courage. Always stand up for what you believe in. Never back down unless you're wrong. If a man insults you, turn the other cheek. If he insults you again, kill him. Make courage your watchword. But courage is more than arms and legs. It takes courage to be yourself, so do it. Above all things, live a life of honor. Honor the people you love, the ideals you cherish and the man inside you.

D'ARTAGNAN. I promise.

FATHER. Now a few parting gifts and you're on your way. Twenty-five crowns. Say nothing. I wish it were more. Second, a letter, recommending you to Monsieur de Treville.

D'ARTAGNAN. Your old friend.

FATHER. Now Captain of the Musketeers.

D'ARTAGNAN. Oh I know. They say that he's fought hundreds of duels in the king's service. They say the king relies on him for everything. They say –

FATHER. "They say, they say." He was my schoolmate. We were lads together, and he will help you thread the needle of Paris. Now keep this safe.

D'ARTAGNAN. Yes, Father.

FATHER. Third, I want to give you...

> *(He gets tears in his eyes.)*

I want you to have something that...

> *(He can hardly speak from emotion.)*

It's my beloved...

> *(He takes a hat out of his bag and puts it on* **D'ARTAGNAN**'s *head. It is an old, worn-out provincial hat with a wide brim, turned up in front, with frazzled piping and a red feather sticking out the side.)*

D'ARTAGNAN. Your hat?

FATHER. The hat I wore in Paris, in the Tuilleries, defending the king and queen with my life.

D'ARTAGNAN. Sir –

FATHER. On parade with my fellow musketeers, standing handsomely in the brilliant sun –

D'ARTAGNAN. But sir –

FATHER. And then in battle, in the heat of the fray, it took musket-fire –

D'ARTAGNAN. But sir, it looks ridiculous.

FATHER. What?

D'ARTAGNAN. It looks…ridiculously handsome and I cannot take it from you, it would be unkind.

FATHER. No, no. I want you to have it. I am your father. No sacrifice too great, no gift too large, no hopes too grand, no heart too noble.

D'ARTAGNAN. Lucky me, dear father.

> (*D'Artagnan's* **MOTHER**, *Cecile, bustles in, her apron to her mouth, almost incoherent with grief at her son's departure.*)

MOTHER. Oh, D'Artagnan! I've packed plenty of food for your journey, extra stockings, and my special ointment in case you get yourself w-w-wounded.

> (*She bursts into tears and clutches her son.*)

> (*In the following speech,* **FATHER** *is referring to his old hat, but* **D'ARTAGNAN** *thinks he's referring to his mother.*)

FATHER I remember the old girl when I first found her.

D'ARTAGNAN. Father!

FATHER. And now your mother and I have a surprise for you. Sabine!

> (**SABINE** *enters, carrying a valise.*)

Are you ready?

SABINE. To take on the world, Father. My bags are packed, my affairs in order, and I look on life as my own small oyster.

D'ARTAGNAN. What's going on?

FATHER. Sabine is going with you to Paris.

D'ARTAGNAN. What?!

FATHER. I've arranged for her schooling. She's my daughter. I want her to continue her education, and I want you to protect her on the way.

D'ARTAGNAN. But I'll – I'll look ridiculous, entering Paris with a little sister. And I'll have enough to worry about without playing nursemaid to some...

SABINE. I trust, Brother, that I shall be no burden to you, but rather do your bidding as you require.

> (**FATHER** *and* **MOTHER** *turn to* **D'ARTAGNAN** *as if to say, "Do you see?" With her parents turned away,* **SABINE** *sticks out her tongue and makes a face at* **D'ARTAGNAN**.)

D'ARTAGNAN. That's it, I'll kill her –

> (**D'ARTAGNAN** *chases* **SABINE** *until* **FATHER** *grabs him.*)

FATHER. Do you do as I ask?! Or do you dishonor the ancient name "D'Artagnan"?

D'ARTAGNAN. As you wish, Father.

FATHER. Fine then. Be off with you.

> (*Fond farewells are exchanged. As* **D'ARTAGNAN** *hugs his* **MOTHER**, **FATHER** *once again refers to his old hat.*)

Maybe a bit too wide and worn out, but she's a good old girl.

> (**D'ARTAGNAN**, **SABINE**, *and* **MOTHER** *all look puzzled.* **MOTHER** *and* **FATHER** *exit.*)

SABINE. Turn around.

D'ARTAGNAN. What? ...What are you doing?

SABINE. (*Changing clothes.*) What does it look like I'm doing? It's dangerous between here and Paris. I can't very well go as a woman.

D'ARTAGNAN. But I'm protecting you. That's the point!

SABINE. You? Protect me? Ha. And why should you have all the fun? I'm as good a swordsman as you are any day of the week.

D'ARTAGNAN. Oh, please.

SABINE. "Oh, please." And they want me to go to a convent school. You know being a girl in the seventeenth century is just not that much fun. There.

(She is now dressed as a young man.)

Now call me – what's a good name for a French servant?

D'ARTAGNAN. Brioche.

SABINE. What about Planchet? I heard it in a story once; it was all about honor and romance.

(In a man's voice, bowing.) "Planchet. At your service, sir."

D'ARTAGNAN. Oh, Lord...

SABINE. Would you cheer up?! This is just the kind of adventure we dreamed about in the back garden, don't you remember? Fighting injustice. Hya! Hya! Defending the king and queen. Now hurry up! And bring my bag! I want to meet some real musketeers and fall in love with one of them!

> *(**SABINE** runs off. **D'ARTAGNAN** picks up her valise and follows her, shaking his head. As he goes, two musket shots ring out – Bang! Bang! – and we're suddenly in:)*

Scene Two

(Outside the cardinal's palace, at night. **ATHOS**, **PORTHOS**, *and* **ARAMIS**, *three of the king's musketeers, are revealed dramatically. Then we hear the voice of* **CARDINAL RICHELIEU** *screaming from offstage.)*

CARDINAL RICHELIEU. *(Offstage.) Stop them! Somebody stop those musketeers!*

PORTHOS. Let's get out of here, quick!

ARAMIS. Athos, I don't think this was advisable.

PORTHOS. That's the understatement of the year.

ATHOS. It was symbolic.

ARAMIS. You call this symbolic?

PORTHOS. Stealing the cardinal's nightcap?

(He holds it up.)

ATHOS. It's a reminder.

PORTHOS. A reminder of what? That he's bald?

ATHOS. A reminder that he's not invulnerable.

ARAMIS. Athos –

ATHOS. That he isn't the only power in France.

ARAMIS. Athos –

ATHOS. That the king is the king and that we're his champions.

ARAMIS. Athos!

ATHOS. What?

ARAMIS. We're surrounded.

ATHOS. Oh, bugger.

ROCHEFORT. *(Offstage.)* Get those musketeers!

(Bang! Bang! Bang! Musket balls fly at them from every direction.)

ARAMIS. Quickly!

ATHOS. Go!

PORTHOS. Retreat!

(As the **MUSKETEERS** *run off,* **CARDINAL RICHELIEU** *appears in his sleeping robe – but without his nightcap.* **ROCHEFORT**, *his henchman, is with him.* **ROCHEFORT** *wears an eyepatch.)*

CARDINAL RICHELIEU. Stop them you fool! You're the Captain of my Guard, for heaven's sake!

ROCHEFORT. We tried, Your Eminence. They slipped away.

CARDINAL RICHELIEU. Then track them down to where they live!

ROCHEFORT. We don't know where they live. That's the problem. The famous "Three Musketeers" and we can never find them.

CARDINAL RICHELIEU. Those reprobates, those interfering, overstuffed vermin! *They were in my room!*

ROCHEFORT. There's another issue, Sire. Turn around.

CARDINAL RICHELIEU. What?

(The **CARDINAL** *turns around and we see the back of his robe has been cut away, revealing his underwear.)*

I really hate them.

(The **CARDINAL** *stalks off in high dudgeon, as we enter:)*

Scene Three

(The ancient town of Mauriac, the next morning. As the set changes, **D'ARTAGNAN** *and* **SABINE** *enter.)*

SABINE. We're almost to Paris, just a few more miles. I'll bet you're glad I came, aren't you. Thanks to me we didn't make one wrong turn, not a single one.
(Reading a sign.) "Town of Mauriac. Population: forty-seven. New business welcome." Look! There's an inn! I'm starving, I'll be inside. Take my bag.

D'ARTAGNAN. Hey, wait a second, you're the servant!

(Too late. She's gone. Two men enter as **SABINE** *exits:* **ROCHEFORT** *and* **RAVANCHE**, *Rochefort's servant, a bully.)*

RAVANCHE. God's blood! Would you look at that hat! Ha!

ROCHEFORT. Christ, that's not a hat, it's a cry for help.

RAVANCHE. And look at the feather!

ROCHEFORT. That's not a feather, it's a chicken bone.

ROCHEFORT & RAVANCHE. Hahahahahahaha!

D'ARTAGNAN. You there. What are you laughing at?

ROCHEFORT. Me, sir?

D'ARTAGNAN. When I see a man laughing, I like to be told the joke so that I can laugh too.

ROCHEFORT. I was not talking to you, sir.

D'ARTAGNAN. No, but I am talking to you, sir. Do you laugh at me, sir?

ROCHEFORT. I laugh at your hat, sir. Unless I'm mistaken and it's not a hat but a chicken that perched on your head before dying.

D'ARTAGNAN. Turn and face me or I'll run you through!

ROCHEFORT. Run me through? Me? Are you mad? Ravanche, kill this puppy.

*(**RAVANCHE** and **D'ARTAGNAN** fight. **D'ARTAGNAN** stabs, and **ROCHEFORT** joins them. Then **MILADY**, the Countess de Winter,*

enters behind **D'ARTAGNAN** *and hits him over the head with a jug.* **D'ARTAGNAN** *sinks to the ground, unconscious.)*

(**MILADY** *is the most dangerous woman in Europe. Her cunning is legendary. She's remarkably beautiful and wears strong, stunning clothes. She never utters an ill-chosen word.)*

MILADY. See to my horses.

(**RAVANCHE** *exits.)*

ROCHEFORT. Should I thank you for that?

MILADY. You should thank me for living because I allow you to do it. Now who's the boy? He looks a cut above the local dregs.

ROCHEFORT. I have no idea. He has a chip on his shoulder, I'll tell you that. What are you doing?

(**MILADY** *is going through* **D'ARTAGNAN**'s *pockets.)*

MILADY. I like to know my enemies. Knowledge is power and power is life.

ROCHEFORT. Who said that?

MILADY. I did, you idiot.

ROCHEFORT. He's a country bumpkin.

MILADY. A bumpkin. I see. Just a country bumpkin, with a letter to Monsieur de Treville in his pocket.

ROCHEFORT. Treville? Let me see that...

(**ROCHEFORT** *reaches for the letter, but* **MILADY** *pulls a concealed dagger from her dress, pointing it at his throat. This dagger will make several appearances in the play, and whenever* **MILADY** *pulls it out, it appears instantly, with a snap.)*

MILADY. I'm not quite finished with it, am I?

ROCHEFORT. Why are you here, Milady?

MILADY. To give you a message from Cardinal Richelieu. Tomorrow at noon a young woman named Constance Bonacieux will be in the Rue Hachette carrying certain letters. The cardinal wants them at any cost. Is that clear?

ROCHEFORT. Yes, ma'am.

MILADY. There, you may have the letter now. Show it to the cardinal. Perhaps he'll give you a promotion and you can eat at the grown-ups' table. Let's go.

>   (**ROCHEFORT** *snatches up the letter. Then raises his sword to kill* **D'ARTAGNAN**.)

No, you fool! This is no time to draw attention to yourself. Besides, he's pretty. I may want him someday for a house pet.

>   (*She kisses* **D'ARTAGNAN** *on the lips. As she does, he starts to regain consciousness.*)

D'ARTAGNAN. Hello...

>   (*Wham! She hits him viciously on the side of the head and knocks him out again.* **ROCHEFORT** *gapes.*)

MILADY. Close your mouth, and follow me.

>   (**MILADY** *exits.* **ROCHEFORT** *looks at* **D'ARTAGNAN** *with hatred. Then he breaks* **D'ARTAGNAN***'s sword in half and leaves. As he goes,* **SABINE** *comes out of the inn.*)

SABINE. D'Arty, I got us some wine and sausage for the trip and I thought we could... D'Arty, what happened?! Say something!

>   (**D'ARTAGNAN** *groans.*)

D'ARTAGNAN. Oh Sabine, she's so beautiful!

>   (*Music* plays, which takes us into:*)

---

*A license to produce *The Three Musketeers* does not include a performance license for any third-party or copyrighted music. Licensees should create an original composition or use music in the public domain. For further information, please see Music Use Note on page 3.

Scene Four

(The reception room of Monsieur de Treville's house in Paris, the next day. The house is legendary as the training camp for the king's musketeers. There isn't a boy in the world who wouldn't give a year of his life to visit this place. Immediately we hear **MONSIEUR DE TREVILLE**, *screaming out a window at the top of his lungs. He's the most impatient man in Paris.)*

TREVILLE. Aramis! Aramis, get in here! And bring your two reprobate friends in with you!

*(**ARAMIS** and **PORTHOS** join **TREVILLE**. We now have a moment to examine the **MUSKETEERS** more closely. **ARAMIS** is strikingly handsome and has genuine hopes for a future in the church. Two things, however, stand in his way: he has a hot temper, which can flare at any moment, and he loves to be around beautiful women.)*

*(**PORTHOS**, meanwhile, is Bacchus brought to life, but with a good heart. He's extremely vain and quite a dandy, but since he's one of the three greatest swordsmen in all of France, he can afford to be.)*

ARAMIS. Monsieur de Treville, let me explain.

TREVILLE. Explain? Why you'd better explain!

PORTHOS. Aramis, let *me* explain.

ARAMIS. I said I'll do it!

TREVILLE. And it better be good.

ARAMIS. Well, sir, it happened like this –

PORTHOS. There were four hundred of them! They had dogs, and guns, and some of the dogs had guns –

ARAMIS. Porthos.

TREVILLE. My three greatest musketeers, bested by the cardinal's guards.

ARAMIS. That's not exactly –

TREVILLE. Do you understand the humiliation I feel?

ARAMIS. Yes but –

TREVILLE. The shame the king himself is feeling?

ARAMIS. But if you'll –

TREVILLE. The sneers he has had to endure from the cardinal?

ARAMIS. *May I please say something?!*

TREVILLE. Wait. Where's Athos?

(**PORTHOS** *and* **ARAMIS** *glance at each other.*)

PORTHOS. Well, let's see, I think he's visiting his uncle –

ARAMIS. He's sick.

PORTHOS. His sick uncle. The poor old man has the plague –

ARAMIS. A cold –

PORTHOS. It's a form of the plague that starts as a cold. You begin by sneezing, then suddenly you're lying there dead as a mackerel.

TREVILLE. What are you talking about? Porthos, would you stop this tomfoolery? Now where's Athos?!

ATHOS. I'm right here.

(**ATHOS** *walks in. He's gravely intelligent, full of shadows, with the courage of a lion, and more dangerous than the others. At the moment, however, he's badly wounded, and his right arm has a blood-soaked bandage on it.*)

TREVILLE. My good man, you're hurt.

ATHOS. A flesh wound –

TREVILLE. Tell me what happened.

ARAMIS. We were ambushed by the cardinal's guards.

PORTHOS. They were angry about a little trick we pulled and they called for help. Eh?

ATHOS. Ow!

PORTHOS. Sorry.

ARAMIS. But we got the hat.

TREVILLE. Fetch my doctor and get this wound dressed properly. And next time tell me the truth from the beginning.

ARAMIS. Only God knows the truth and He keeps it a secret.

*(As **TREVILLE** shoos the **MUSKETEERS** out the door, we see **D'ARTAGNAN** in the doorway, about to knock.)*

D'ARTAGNAN. Oh, excuse me, sir. I-I have an appointment. They told me to come right up.

TREVILLE. Come in, come in. And lads, you did very well. I'm proud of you.

PORTHOS. *(At the door.)* Is that an apology?

TREVILLE. Get out.

PORTHOS. It sounded surprisingly like an apology to me.

TREVILLE. I said get out.

PORTHOS. And yet I didn't hear those magic words, "I'm sorry, Porthos" –

TREVILLE. Get out, get out, get out!

*(They exit, and he wheels on **D'ARTAGNAN**.)*

Now what do you want?

D'ARTAGNAN. I-I've come for an interview, sir. To be a musketeer. I'm good with a sword, I promise you that. Of course I realize you're called *musket*-teers, and I've never shot a musket myself, but I bet I'd be good with one if I tried it. Which I haven't. But I would be. You'd be amazed.

TREVILLE. *(Amused at youth.)* You sound like you're from Gascony.

D'ARTAGNAN. I am, sir. I arrived today with my sister – my servant. I-I call him sister because we were raised together and he sometimes wears a dress. When he's alone. So he tells me.

TREVILLE. And you want to be a musketeer?

D'ARTAGNAN. Yes sir. My father wrote me a letter of introduction. He's an old friend of yours. D'Artagnan de Beaugency.

TREVILLE. D'Artagnan? Ha. Well what do you know. How's he doing?

D'ARTAGNAN. He's well, sir, and sends his regards.

TREVILLE. And it looks like he sent his old hat as well. We wore these in the Tuilleries defending the king and queen. Let's see that letter of yours.

D'ARTAGNAN. I'm afraid I lost it. I mean it was taken from me. And then this beautiful goddess kissed me, and then the man with the eyepatch must have kicked me because I was very sore – but I would have beaten him soundly in a fair fight, I promise you that. I have been a swordsman since I was six years old. Hya!

(He jumps into the "en garde" position and draws his sword – but thanks to Rochefort, the blade is only five inches long.)

TREVILLE. No letter. Broken sword. Manservant who wears a dress. But you have your father's hat. Here's what I'll do. I'll offer you a commission in the King's Regiment. It's not the musketeers, I grant you, but no one starts there anyway. You've got to work your way up to it. Prove yourself in some campaign or other. Show skill and valor in the king's service –

*(***D'ARTAGNAN*** has seen ***ROCHEFORT*** in the street.)*

And are you listening to me?!

D'ARTAGNAN. That's him! Just walking there! The man who took my letter! I need a sword. May I borrow this?

(Takes one of Treville's swords from the wall.)

I'll return it, I promise. Thank you so much, you're very kind. I'll call again!

*(To ***TREVILLE***'s surprise, ***D'ARTAGNAN*** leaps out of the window and rushes after the man with the eyepatch. We follow ***D'ARTAGNAN*** out of the chamber and into:)*

Scene Five

(The street below. **D'ARTAGNAN** *looks desperately in both directions to catch a glimpse of Rochefort. He darts in one direction – and runs straight into* **ATHOS**.*)*

ATHOS. *(His wound.)* Ow!

D'ARTAGNAN. Oh dear. Are you all right?

ATHOS. Do I look all right?!

D'ARTAGNAN. I'm awfully sorry, but I have to hurry.

ATHOS. You're "sorry"?

D'ARTAGNAN. Yes.

ATHOS. And that's all you have to say?

D'ARTAGNAN. What else can I say? It was an accident. But honestly, I've got to run, there's this man with an eyepatch and I've got to kill him.

ATHOS. *(Turns away.)* Obviously from the country.

D'ARTAGNAN. What? What did you say?

ATHOS. I said you're from the country.

D'ARTAGNAN. So what if I am? Are you implying something?

ATHOS. I'm implying that you have country manners, boy. You're in Paris now, so try to improve them.

D'ARTAGNAN. My manners, sir, are as good as yours. And I'm very proud of where I come from, and perhaps that's saying more than you are.

ATHOS. Was that an insult?

D'ARTAGNAN. It was meant to be.

ATHOS. Shall we settle it now?

D'ARTAGNAN. I can't right now because I'm chasing someone. Name the time.

ATHOS. Ten this evening, behind the Luxembourg.

D'ARTAGNAN. Done.

(**D'ARTAGNAN** *slaps* **ATHOS** *on the arm to seal the bargain.)*

ATHOS. Ow!

D'ARTAGNAN. Oh sorry. Do you fight right-handed, by the way?

ATHOS. I do, but I'm even better with my left, so I suggest you book a church for the funeral.

> (**ATHOS** *exits. At the same moment* **PORTHOS** *enters from the other direction, showing off his newest cloak to a female admirer named* **ADELE**. *Meanwhile,* **D'ARTAGNAN** *is looking up and down the street for Rochefort.*)

PORTHOS. Silk. Pure silk from India. One of a kind. Ha ha!

ADELE. Really?

PORTHOS. Takes months and months to make a piece like this. Feel it. Right here. Light as a feather, but strong as chain mail.

ADELE. Oh, Porthos.

PORTHOS. Made from an ancient dye, you see. From the bark of puzzle trees and the petals of little spiced roses. Just look at the colors.

> (*He takes one end of the cloak and spins around, causing it to billow out like a sail. As he does,* **D'ARTAGNAN** *cries out, thinking he's spotted Rochefort in the distance.*)

D'ARTAGNAN. Hey!

> (*He darts past* **PORTHOS** *but accidentally gets caught up in the cloak. It covers him like a bed sheet and he can't see a thing. He gropes for light and tears the cloak off* **PORTHOS**, *ending up in a heap on the ground.*)

(*Disentangling himself.*) I-I'm sorry! I was in a hurry!

PORTHOS. You crack-brained codfish! You-you-you pop-eyed little clam! Look what you've done!

D'ARTAGNAN. I'll pay for it, sir. I swear. I-I have some money. But right now if I could just –

PORTHOS. Oh you will pay for it indeed, I promise you. It was brand new. And it looked stunning on me! Do you think that garments like this grow on trees?!

D'ARTAGNAN. Sir, I'm very –

PORTHOS. Forty crowns.

D'ARTAGNAN. What?

PORTHOS. Fifty crowns. That's what you owe me.

D'ARTAGNAN. For this old thing?

PORTHOS. Sixty crowns. It's one of a kind.

D'ARTAGNAN. Oh come now, sir. I saw capes like this on the stalls by the river. They wanted one crown fifty and I said it was too much.

PORTHOS. I believe you're mistaken.

D'ARTAGNAN. Oh I don't think so. There was a whole pile of them. They looked identical.

> (**ADELE** *laughs and walks off.*)

PORTHOS. Adele, wait! It's from the bark of puzzle trees... and the petals of little...spiced roses...

> (*She's gone;* **PORTHOS** *turns back to* **D'ARTAGNAN**, *furious.*)

You are a puppy, sir. An imbecile. And I demand satisfaction. Do you agree, or do you cower in fear?

D'ARTAGNAN. A "D'Artagnan" never cowers, sir. Name the time.

PORTHOS. Eleven o'clock. Behind the Luxembourg.

D'ARTAGNAN. I'll be there.

> (**PORTHOS** *exits.* **D'ARTAGNAN** *calls after him:*)

And if you need a new cloak, try the stalls near the river! They're a crown fifty!

> (**PORTHOS** *is gone.* **D'ARTAGNAN** *is alone now.*)

And thanks to you, I lost the one-eyed man. Achoo! And now I've got a cold...and I'm going to die at ten o'clock. Or eleven if I get lucky.

> (*We hear a silvery laugh and* **ARAMIS** *enters down the street with a beautiful girl on his arm. Her name is* **ELISE**, *and they're both flirting like mad.*)

ELISE. Aramis, stop it! You're making me blush! I thought you were taking holy orders.

ARAMIS. I am, my darling. The Church is my life. "And the sinful world that appears before us will perish into dust like a mirage of longing." Isaiah, Chapter Forty-five.

ELISE. Oh, Aramis...

>*(She drops her handkerchief, quite deliberately, in flirtation.)*

D'ARTAGNAN. Achoo!

>*(Without thinking,* **D'ARTAGNAN** *picks up the handkerchief and blows his nose in it.)*

ARAMIS. Sir!

D'ARTAGNAN. Yes?

ARAMIS. I believe that is the Lady's handkerchief.

D'ARTAGNAN. It is? Oh. I beg your pardon. I-I wasn't thinking. Here.

>*(He tries to hand it back to* **ELISE***.)*

ELISE. Ah!

ARAMIS. Get back!

D'ARTAGNAN. Oh, sorry. Sorry! I-I could have it cleaned for you, how's that? And return it tomorrow. Or I could wash it in one of the fountains here.

ELISE. Aramis, do something!

ARAMIS. Sir, you have insulted the very name of womanhood.

D'ARTAGNAN. Did I? I thought I just blew my nose.

ARAMIS. Are you being funny?

D'ARTAGNAN. I didn't think so.

ARAMIS. I believe you're being funny, sir, and I don't like it *and I demand satisfaction*!

D'ARTAGNAN. Don't tell me. Behind the Luxembourg at twelve o'clock.

ARAMIS. No, eleven.

D'ARTAGNAN. It'll have to be twelve, I'm booked at eleven.

ARAMIS. Fine. Twelve o'clock. And don't be late.

D'ARTAGNAN. Done.

"And he shall enter th͟   ͟͟   ;
                    dow of d͟   "

D'ARTAGNAN. "And he shall pull down his trousers and then shall he stick out his backside." D'Artagnan, Chapter Twelve.

>   (**ARAMIS** *stamps his foot in rage and exits with* **ELISE.** **D'ARTAGNAN** *is alone again.*)

God in heaven. I'm as good as dead. Is this why I trained with my father all those years? Is this why he taught me everything he knows? About life? About honor? Is this what honor means? He taught me there are some things worth dying for, and I would die for them in an instant, but dying because I blew my nose in a blue hankie?

>   (**SABINE** *runs in.*)

SABINE. D'Arty, there you are! Guess what, guess what?! I found us a room for less than a crown a night! It isn't much, but it has a window. And wait'll you see Paris, D'Arty. It's wonderful! There's people everywhere, and taverns and brawling... Are you all right? Did you see Treville? Are you a musketeer yet?

D'ARTAGNAN. Not yet, dear sister. Someday, perhaps, if I live that long.

SABINE. What do you mean?

D'ARTAGNAN. Never mind. Come along. Let's get you to that school of yours.

SABINE. I don't want to go.

D'ARTAGNAN. Sabine –

SABINE. Not yet! I want to see more of Paris first.

D'ARTAGNAN. Sabine, it's time for school!

SABINE. No! You'll have to catch me first!

>   (*She darts one way, then another, then runs down the street. As he chases her, he runs into*

a beautiful young woman who's running for her life. Her name is **CONSTANCE BONACIEUX***.)*

CONSTANCE. Help me, sir, please! Two men are after me.

(Before **D'ARTAGNAN** *can speak,* **RAVANCHE** *runs in like a madman, sword drawn, trying to stop* **CONSTANCE** *at any price.)*

D'ARTAGNAN. Stay behind me.

(He draws his sword.)

RAVANCHE. You there. Stand aside.

D'ARTAGNAN. What do you want?

RAVANCHE. I want to speak with the young lady.

D'ARTAGNAN. But the young lady doesn't want to speak with you.

RAVANCHE. Monsieur, if I was you, I wouldn't meddle in this.

D'ARTAGNAN. And if I were you, I wouldn't tell me what to do.

*(***RAVANCHE** *attacks.* **D'ARTAGNAN** *defends himself while keeping* **CONSTANCE** *away from the brute.)*

CONSTANCE. Look out! Here comes the other one!

*(***ROCHEFORT** *enters.)*

D'ARTAGNAN. You!

ROCHEFORT. Oh my God, it's the puppy. I should have killed you yesterday.

D'ARTAGNAN. You're going to wish you had. Now give me the letter!

ROCHEFORT. Come and get it.

(The three men fight. It's hair-raising. **D'ARTAGNAN** *holds them off. Then, with a magnificent thrust, he pierces* **RAVANCHE***, who howls with pain. Now it's* **D'ARTAGNAN** *vs.* **ROCHEFORT***, who grabs* **CONSTANCE***. She screams and struggles to get away.)*

D'ARTAGNAN. Let her go!

> (**CONSTANCE** *bites* **ROCHEFORT**'s *hand and he screams with agony.* **D'ARTAGNAN** *pursues the advantage like a demon and runs* **ROCHEFORT** *through the side. Instinctively,* **CONSTANCE** *runs to* **D'ARTAGNAN** *and clings to him for protection.*)

ROCHEFORT. I'm going to kill you for this.

> (**ROCHEFORT** *and* **RAVANCHE**, *both wounded, make a run for it, leaving* **D'ARTAGNAN** *and* **CONSTANCE** *alone.*)

D'ARTAGNAN. Are you all right?

CONSTANCE. Yes, thank you.

D'ARTAGNAN. Why were they after you?

CONSTANCE. They want to kill me because I serve the queen.

D'ARTAGNAN. The queen?

CONSTANCE. Yes. I must go to her at once. I carry a letter for her that she must see. She'll be sick with worry.

D'ARTAGNAN. What's your name?

CONSTANCE. Constance. Constance Bonacieux. What's yours?

D'ARTAGNAN. D'Artagnan.

CONSTANCE. Thank you...D'Artagnan. I'm in your debt.

D'ARTAGNAN. *(Shy.)* It was nothing.

> (*They're both in love.*)

CONSTANCE. I must leave now.

D'ARTAGNAN. Will you be safe?

CONSTANCE. I haven't far to go.

D'ARTAGNAN. And this letter that you carry for the queen. Is it valuable?

CONSTANCE. It is to her. It's from one she loves.

D'ARTAGNAN. Then it's dangerous.

CONSTANCE. All matters of the heart are dangerous. Because hearts can break. I must go.

D'ARTAGNAN. Wait! Will I see you again? I must. Please.

(She kisses him.)

CONSTANCE. Tonight at one o'clock, behind the Luxembourg.

(She runs off. **D'ARTAGNAN** *touches his lips in wonder. As he does, the scene changes to:)*

Scene Six

*(A garden on the grounds of the royal palace,
a few minutes later. We're in the clearing of a
maze. As the lights come up, we see **KING LOUIS
XIII** and **QUEEN ANNE OF AUSTRIA** playing
chess. **QUEEN ANNE** is a handsome woman in
her thirties, sweet-natured and intelligent.
At the moment she looks apprehensive and
frequently glances at one of the entrances.
KING LOUIS, also in his thirties, is absorbed in
the game. He says some silly things at times
and gets confused, but he's trying hard to live
up to his title.)*

KING LOUIS. I put myself in check and you didn't notice.

QUEEN ANNE. What?

KING LOUIS. What are you so distracted about? I'm-I'm the King of France. You have to pay attention!

QUEEN ANNE. I'm sorry, Louis. I'll try

KING LOUIS. It's not just a game, you know. It's-it's-it's symbolic. Look. King. Queen. Bishop. Knight. It's all about us, you see – the king and the queen. The knight is the soldier, and the bishop represents the church – though he should be called the cardinal, shouldn't he? Cardinal Richelieu. But you notice that he's below you in the hierarchy, not above you, and you've got to remember that.

QUEEN ANNE. As do you, my love.

KING LOUIS. I know. I know. It's just that he makes it so difficult sometimes. Always pretending he's smarter than I am. His guards beating my guards. I hate that.

*(At this moment **CARDINAL RICHELIEU** walks
in, wearing the deep red, flowing robes of a
cardinal in the Catholic Church.)*

CARDINAL RICHELIEU. *(To the **QUEEN**.)* Well, well, well. How delightful to see you. You're looking radiant.

KING LOUIS. Hello, Cardinal. Ignoring me today, are we?

CARDINAL RICHELIEU. Not in the least, Sire. You're looking well. Have you had good news?

KING LOUIS. No. As a matter of fact I've had disturbing news. I understand that your guards took advantage of my musketeers this morning and I want it to stop.

CARDINAL RICHELIEU. "Took advantage"? Now what does that mean?

KING LOUIS. Ganged up. Outnumbered. Then started brawling on some pretext or other.

CARDINAL RICHELIEU. Forgive me, Sire, but my guards were merely doing their duty, preventing a duel, which I do believe is against the law, is it not?

KING LOUIS. Well, yes. But it's a technicality. You know it is.

CARDINAL RICHELIEU. I know that I love the law, Your Grace, if that's what you mean.

KING LOUIS. That's not exactly what I mean, now is it?

CARDINAL RICHELIEU. I wouldn't know, Your Majesty, as I don't have the advantage of being inside your Majesty's... spacious brain.

KING LOUIS. "Spacious"?

CARDINAL RICHELIEU. Admirably large, Your Highness.

KING LOUIS. May I make a suggestion? Keep your guards away from my musketeers, or you might find yourself with a little spaciousness in your own brain. Since you admire that quality so highly.

(The **KING** *exits.)*

CARDINAL RICHELIEU. The king is unhappy.

QUEEN ANNE. He faces the strain of running the country.

CARDINAL RICHELIEU. And yet he doesn't really run the country, does he? He plays with his little toys. He builds fountains in gardens.

QUEEN ANNE. How dare you speak of the king this way!

CARDINAL RICHELIEU. "How dare I, how dare I." Yes, yes, yes. I've heard it all before. But look at you. You're magnificent. You need a consort. Someone better than that English Buckingham fellow.

QUEEN ANNE. Buckingham?

CARDINAL RICHELIEU. The Duke of Buckingham is your lover, I believe?

QUEEN ANNE. I-I don't know what you're talking about.

CARDINAL RICHELIEU. Oh, please. Don't insult me. I've had you under observation since the day you arrived here from Austria with your little of Sachertorte.

QUEEN ANNE. How dare you! I'm the queen!

CARDINAL RICHELIEU. Indeed you are. And you've been writing and receiving love letters with an English duke, and exchanging them through your lady-in-waiting.

QUEEN ANNE. You're insane.

CARDINAL RICHELIEU. Am I? And am I insane to dream of what you and I could accomplish together? Just think of the power we'd have together. The people love you and they fear me. Could there be a more perfect combination?

(He strokes her cheek and Whap! She slaps him hard across the face.)

Ouch.

QUEEN ANNE. I'll call the guard! I-I'll have you hanged!

CARDINAL RICHELIEU. Fine. Go ahead. What are you waiting for? Your little friend Constance Bonancieux?

QUEEN ANNE. *(Frightened.)* Constance?

CARDINAL RICHELIEU. Loyal handmaid and conspicuous go-between. That's a very dangerous combination, you know.

QUEEN ANNE. *Constance?*

CARDINAL RICHELIEU. If I were you I'd save your breath. By now she's probably lying in a gutter with a sword through her chest.

*(With a cry of desperation, the **QUEEN** runs to the opening in the hedge.)*

QUEEN ANNE. *Constance!*

> *(Just as she gets there, **CONSTANCE** enters.)*

CONSTANCE. Yes, my lady?

> *(The **CARDINAL** turns, thunderstruck.)*

CARDINAL RICHELIEU. What?

QUEEN ANNE. Oh, thank God! Are you all right?!

CONSTANCE. Of course, my lady.

QUEEN ANNE. I thought you were –

CONSTANCE. I'm fine, I assure you. And the package we discussed – I have it right here.

QUEEN ANNE. Oh thank heavens.

ROCHEFORT. *(Offstage.)* Eminence. Your Eminence!

> *(**ROCHEFORT** runs in, then sees the **QUEEN**.)*

Oh forgive me, Your Highness. I apologize. They didn't tell me that you were –

QUEEN ANNE. That's quite all right. The cardinal is all yours. I wouldn't dream of keeping him.

> *(This last with specific meaning. She and **CONSTANCE** exit.)*

ROCHEFORT. I'm sorry to interrupt, Your Grace, but I thought you should ARGHHHH!

> *(The **CARDINAL** has grabbed **ROCHEFORT** by the throat and is, quite literally, choking him to death.)*

CARDINAL RICHELIEU. You fool! You incompetent bungler!

ROCHEFORT. *(Gurgling.)* Your Grace... Please...

CARDINAL RICHELIEU. Please what? Please stop choking you? No, I think I'll keep it up.

ROCHEFORT. Arggghhh! It wasn't my fault! Some man came out of nowhere! He must have known in advance.

CARDINAL RICHELIEU. That's impossible.

ROCHEFORT. That's what I thought, but there he was! Argh!

CARDINAL RICHELIEU. What's his name?

ROCHEFORT. His name is D'Artagnan. I encountered him yesterday and he had this letter.

> *(He manages to pull out the letter from D'Artagnan's father. The* **CARDINAL** *releases his grasp and takes the letter.* **ROCHEFORT** *staggers back, gasping for air.)*

CARDINAL RICHELIEU. Bring him to me. Instantly.

ROCHEFORT. Yes, Your Grace. But I'm not sure I know exactly where to – Argggghh.

CARDINAL RICHELIEU. *BRING HIM TO ME OR I'LL HAVE YOUR HEAD!!*

ROCHEFORT. Yes sir. Right away.

> *(***ROCHEFORT*** *begins to exit, holding his side where he was wounded. He lets out a moan.)*

CARDINAL RICHELIEU. Does it hurt?

ROCHEFORT. Yes, Your Grace.

CARDINAL RICHELIEU. Good.

> *(A bell tolls the hour of ten – and now we're at:)*

Scene Seven

(Luxembourg Palace, that night. It's dark out, and all is in shadow. As the bell tolls, we see that we're on a terrace behind the famous palace, which looms up in the background. Statues dot the terrace. **ATHOS** *is sitting, sharpening his sword, as* **D'ARTAGNAN** *enters.)*

D'ARTAGNAN. Who's there?

ATHOS. Who wants to know?

D'ARTAGNAN. D'Artagnan. The man you're going to try to kill.

ATHOS. I don't try to kill anyone. They just keep falling on my sword. Do you have seconds?

D'ARTAGNAN. Yes, I have all the time in the world.

ATHOS. *(Amused.)* No, I meant do you have men to back you up. They're called seconds.

D'ARTAGNAN. Oh, I see. No, I'm afraid not. I don't know anyone in Paris yet, except Monsieur de Treville.

ATHOS. Treville? That's awkward. If I kill you, I'll look like a bit of an ogre, won't I.

D'ARTAGNAN. Not really. Not with that wound of yours. How is it, by the way? Because I was thinking, I have an excellent ointment that my mother gave me when I set off for Paris. I suggest you try it. It's very soothing and almost miraculous in its powers, or so it seems to me.

(He holds it out, but **ATHOS** *hesitates.)*

Please.

ATHOS. You're a gentleman.

*(***ATHOS** *begins to apply it.)*

D'ARTAGNAN. Thank you. It will cure you in just three days, I'm sure of it. We could postpone till then, if you'd prefer. Which doesn't mean I'm not prepared to fight you. I'm not afraid. Well, I suppose I am, a little, but it's a matter of honor now that I've accepted your challenge, so I wouldn't dream of shirking it. Especially now, we're so deep in the stream.

ATHOS. "Deep in the stream." That's a Gascon expression.

D'ARTAGNAN. That's right. I'm from Hautefort.

ATHOS. Sarlat.

D'ARTAGNAN. Really? That's amazing. We're almost neighbors.

ATHOS. It's beautiful there. The countryside. Why waste your time in Paris?

D'ARTAGNAN. To be a musketeer. I want to be like you.

ATHOS. Like me? You can do better than that, young man, I promise you.

(**PORTHOS** *and* **ARAMIS** *enter.*)

PORTHOS. Athos, my boy? Is that you?

ATHOS. It's about time. You're late.

(*To* **D'ARTAGNAN**.) These are my seconds.

PORTHOS. I had to change for the occasion. I'm a slave to fashion. Tyrannized by a pair of pumps, but there you are. I'm fighting a duel myself in an hour against some little upstart who got cheeky with me this after– ... Good Lord, it's him. I'm fighting him at eleven.

ARAMIS. And I at twelve.

ATHOS. I've got him at ten.

PORTHOS. Is this a joke, young man?

D'ARTAGNAN. No, sir. I'm sorry. It happened by chance. And if this gentleman kills me, I'll have wasted your time, so I do apologize.

ATHOS. He's very polite.

(*To* **D'ARTAGNAN**.) Well. Let's get to it, shall we?

D'ARTAGNAN. If you're ready.

(**ATHOS** *stands up and flexes his sword.* **D'ARTAGNAN** *draws his sword and loosens up. The two men salute, cross swords, and take a pass at each other.* **D'ARTAGNAN** *parries beautifully, and* **ARAMIS** *and* **PORTHOS** *clap appreciatively.*)

ARAMIS. Well done.

PORTHOS. Very nice, very nice.

ATHOS. Young man, if I don't kill you – and if by some miracle my friends don't either – I'd be happy to make your further acquaintance. You have a good heart.

D'ARTAGNAN. Thank you, sir. It's a musketeer's heart, as I hope to prove someday.

> (*At which moment* **ROCHEFORT** *enters with several of his* **GUARDS** *backing him up.*)

ROCHEFORT. Halt! Dueling is it? It's against the law!

ARAMIS. We're not dueling.

PORTHOS. We're playing tennis.

ATHOS. (*Urgently to* **D'ARTAGNAN**, *whispering.*) Quick! Get out! Make a run for it!

D'ARTAGNAN. But why should I –?

ATHOS. Quickly! Just do as I say!

> (**D'ARTAGNAN** *hurries away – but not far. He lurks nearby in the shadows.*)

ROCHEFORT. I arrest you in the name of His Eminence Cardinal Richelieu. Lay down your swords.

ATHOS. Rochefort. It's Athos. If you turn and go, we'll do the same. There's no need for bloodshed.

ROCHEFORT. I'm not surprised to hear you begging off since I shed your blood this morning.

> (**ATHOS** *moves to punch* **ROCHEFORT**, *but* **PORTHOS** *pulls him back.*)

PORTHOS. Gentlemen, there is no need to fight, let us retire and have a nightcap.

ARAMIS & ATHOS (*Amused.*) Night Cap!

ROCHEFORT. Joke all you want, but you are under arrest.

ARAMIS. (*Sotto voce.*) I intend to die this time, it's better than facing Treville.

ATHOS. With five of them and three of us, you may get your wish.

(The **MUSKETEERS** *draw their swords – at which point* **D'ARTAGNAN**, *to their surprise, steps out of the shadows.)*

D'ARTAGNAN. Wait. I believe you gentlemen are mistaken. You said there are only three of us. I count four.

ARAMIS. Well done.

ATHOS. Good lad.

PORTHOS. Fine boy. I always said so.

ROCHEFORT. D'Artagnan?

(To his men.) That's the man the cardinal wants. You're coming with me.

D'ARTAGNAN. Not on your life, you red-backed cowards! Come and get us! We're ready for you! Yaaaaaaa!

(Swords start clanging and the fight begins. During the battle we see the **THREE MUSKETEERS** *in action for the first time. Each one is a superb fighter, each in a way that reflects his character.* **ATHOS** *is precise and surgical, perhaps the greatest swordsman in all of France.* **ARAMIS** *is romantic about it. He has touches and flourishes that reflect all his great heroes of the past.* **PORTHOS**, *meanwhile, is comic and insouciant. He banters as he fights, distracting his opponents and amusing himself.)*

PORTHOS. *(While dueling.)* Hello, hello. You're looking well...for a man with jaundice... Wait! Do you realize you're fighting with your left hand?! Ha! Made you look!

(Different from all of them is **D'ARTAGNAN**, *who fights like a young tiger, bouncing this way and that, taking on as many opponents as he can.)*

(As the battle warms up, **SABINE** *enters, holding D'Artagnan's hat – which throws a monkey wrench into everything. She's still dressed as a man.)*

SABINE. *D'Arty!*

> (**SABINE** *rushes toward her brother, but a* **GUARD** *makes a vicious cut toward her, which she deftly avoids and goes on the offensive. Then she saves* **ARAMIS** *from a fatal blow.*)

ARAMIS. My thanks.

SABINE. You're welcome.

> (*And she falls in love with him.*)

D'ARTAGNAN. The field is ours!

ALL. Ha ha! / That's the stuff! / Well done! / Well done!

ARAMIS. *(To* **SABINE.***)* My thanks again, sir. Your name?

SABINE. *(In her woman's voice.)* Planchet, at your service sir. Ha haaaa!

ARAMIS. I am Aramis, this is Porthos and that is Athos.

PORTHOS. Is that a boy?

D'ARTAGNAN. Well yes and no. Oh all right. My sister, gentlemen.

THREE MUSKETEERS. Ahhhhh.

ARAMIS. Well that's a relief.

ATHOS. *(To* **D'ARTAGNAN.***)* They were after you, boy. He knew your name.

D'ARTAGNAN. I met him this morning when he laughed at my hat.

> (*He puts it on and they all react.*)

THREE MUSKETEERS. Yuuuu.

ARAMIS. Is it alive?

PORTHOS. I don't think it's breathing.

ATHOS. It looks like a chicken.

ARAMIS. Then I hope it's dead.

ATHOS. I think it's a gopher.

PORTHOS. I don't see a tail.

ARAMIS. But look, it has a little mouth and teeth.

D'ARTAGNAN. *(Drawing his sword.)* Enough!

SABINE. D'Artagnan!

(The **MUSKETEERS** *laugh, and* **D'ARTAGNAN** *joins in.)*

ATHOS. Come. Let's celebrate. I'll buy you a drink.

(With more shouts of joy they begin to go.)

SABINE. May I join you?

ATHOS. All for one –

SABINE. And one for all! Ha ha!

D'ARTAGNAN. That's what I was going to say!

(They go off happily together as tavern music* begins.)

---

*A license to produce *The Three Musketeers* does not include a performance license for any third-party or copyrighted music. Licensees should create an original composition or use music in the public domain. For further information, please see Music Use Note on page 3.

Scene Eight

(A tavern, warm and lively, full of smoke and ale. The **MUSKETEERS** *are singing a drinking song.*)*

PORTHOS. Bring me a wench! I want a wench! Hey, hey, hey, hey!

> *(***SABINE*** approaches* **ARAMIS**, *who is alone. She carries a pitcher of wine and offers to pour him a glass.)*

SABINE. May I? Are you thirsty?

ARAMIS. The Lord's work requires sustenance. How old are you?

SABINE. Eightee– twenty. Two. And a half.

> *(***ARAMIS*** crosses himself before taking a drink.)*

You're very religious.

ARAMIS. I'm studying to be a priest.

SABINE. You are? Really? But that's such a waste. I-I-I mean – oh, you'd have such beautiful children.

ARAMIS.

SABINE. Have you achieved it yet?

ARAMIS. No.

SABINE. Oh good.

> *(At another table:)*

ATHOS. Drink up, boy. Drink up and tell me more of this enchanting creature of yours.

D'ARTAGNAN. There isn't more to tell, I'm afraid. Her name is Constance Bonacieux and when I met her it felt as

---

*A license to produce *The Three Musketeers* does not include a performance license for any third-party or copyrighted music. Licensees should create an original composition or use music in the public domain. For further information, please see Music Use Note on page 3.

though my heart dropped out of my chest to my knees.
I'm meeting her tonight behind the Luxembourg.

ATHOS. Be careful.

D'ARTAGNAN. I'm sorry?

(The tone becomes elegiac.)

ATHOS. Falling in love is a fool's game. It leads to nothing
but regret. And darkness. And the death of hope.

D'ARTAGNAN. It sounds to me like you've had a bad
experience.

ATHOS. Me? No. Not I. It was a friend of mine. He was a
count then, of the province of Quercy.

D'ARTAGNAN. That's not far from where you and I –

ATHOS. He fell in love at the age of twenty-six with a girl of
twenty, as beautiful as the dawn. She was intoxicating,
like wine that fills your senses and makes you happy
to be alive. She lived in a village with her brother, the
local curate. They settled there the year before and no
one asked from whence they'd come. No one bothered,
for she was all good and he was of God. My friend, the
count, he could have seduced the girl or even ravished
her at his will. But no, he was a man of honor – and
he married her. Then he took her to his home and
worshipped her and gave her jewels and carriages and
they were happy. So very happy. Then one day they
were hunting together and she took a fall. The horse
threw her recklessly and she lost consciousness. The
man rushed to help her, and seeing that her riding
habit was tight and stifling, he slit it open with a knife.
And there, on her shoulder, was a fleur-de-lis. She
was branded a whore, a thief, a murderer. And so this
man, this sovereign ruler of his province with rights of
criminal and of civil justice, he tied her hands behind
her back, and with a good stout rope, he hanged her
from a tree.

D'ARTAGNAN. My God. What happened to her brother?

ATHOS. They looked for him but he'd already fled. Later
they learned that he was her lover and accomplice. The

plan was to marry her off to someone rich and live on the proceeds.

D'ARTAGNAN. And what of the man who hanged her?

ATHOS. He changed his name and was never heard from again. But it is said that he has spent his life fighting evil to purge his sin. And now it's time to get drunk.

(To the **TAVERN KEEPER**.*)* More wine! Hey! A stoup of wine!

> *(We return to* **SABINE** *and* **ARAMIS**. **SABINE** *is a little drunk and her speech is slurred.)*

SABINE. Hey, hey, hey, hey! So to continue, when I was a little girl, a teensy, tiny little girl –

> *(She puts her fingers together about three inches apart.)*

My father put a drop of wine in a spoon, and I got very, very drunk. I was adorable. Are you drunk yet?

ARAMIS. No.

SABINE. Oh, bother.

> *(She picks up a large glass of wine and drinks it off in one long swallow.)*

Are you drunk now?

ARAMIS. You should go home.

SABINE. No! I am a woman! I know I don't look it, but these are only clothes! They can be changed!

> *(She starts to cry.)*

And don't you see what's happening? I think I'm... I think I'm falling... I think I'm falling in love with...

> *(She faints.* **ARAMIS** *springs up to catch her, and there is a general hubbub of reaction.)*

D'ARTAGNAN. What is it?! What happened?!

ARAMIS. Too much to drink. You should take her home.

D'ARTAGNAN. Of course, right away, I'll... Oh no. I'm meeting Constance. Oh now what do I do?

ATHOS. We'll take your sister home with us. We have a chair by the fire.

D'ARTAGNAN. But she has school tomorrow. I promised my father.

ATHOS. Where?

D'ARTAGNAN. The Convent of the Sacred Heart on the Rue Bourget.

ATHOS. Don't worry, we'll get her there. Just go. Go!

D'ARTAGNAN. Thank you.

>(**D'ARTAGNAN** *embraces* **ATHOS**, *then leaves the tavern.* **ATHOS** *picks up* **SABINE**, *puts her on his shoulder, and carries her out as the scene changes to:)*

Scene Nine

(Luxembourg Palace, in darkness. As the church bell chimes one o'clock, **CONSTANCE** *hurries in, followed closely by* **SEPTIME**, *the queen's servant, who is trying to stop her.)*

SEPTIME. Madam, no!

CONSTANCE. But I must!

SEPTIME. But the queen is impatient.

CONSTANCE. Just tell her to wait. I...I have an appointment with a young man who saved my life. She'll know what I mean, so please just tell her I'll be there shortly.

D'ARTAGNAN. *(Offstage.)* Constance.

CONSTANCE. Please.

SEPTIME. All right, five minutes.

(He exits into the shadows as **D'ARTAGNAN** *hurries on.)*

D'ARTAGNAN. Constance. I'm sorry I'm late. I was having a duel with a fellow named Athos, who's a lovely chap – we could be excellent friends – he's a musketeer – and then the cardinal's guards arrived and we fought them and won, all four of us fought together, you see, and then we had to celebrate of course in a tavern, and my darling sister was there and she got very drunk –

CONSTANCE. Do you always talk this much?

D'ARTAGNAN. Yes. No. Sorry. You talk now.

CONSTANCE. I have nothing to say. I only wanted to thank you for saving my life. It was very brave.

D'ARTAGNAN. Was it?

CONSTANCE. Yes.

D'ARTAGNAN. Oh. Thank you. I came to Paris to be brave, but I had no idea what I might become until...until I set eyes on you.

CONSTANCE. *(Breathless, gazing into his eyes.)* Really?

SEPTIME. *(Interrupting.)* Madam, I'm afraid it's time to –

CONSTANCE. *GET OUT!*

> (**SEPTIME** *retreats, and* **CONSTANCE** *resumes exactly as before:*)

Really?

D'ARTAGNAN. Yes. You inspired me then, and you still inspire me. The way the moon and the stars inspire me.

SEPTIME. That's a cliché.

D'ARTAGNAN. I know, but I'm not a poet.

(To **CONSTANCE**.*)* I'm just a man whose tongue is tied by your beauty. Who moves in your shadow, breathes in your wake, and lives and dies by your approval.

SEPTIME. That's much better.

D'ARTAGNAN. Who *is* that?

CONSTANCE. A royal servant and a royal pain in the –

SEPTIME. Madam!

CONSTANCE. – Pain in the side of a woman who wishes to thank the man who saved her life.

> *(She kisses* **D'ARTAGNAN** *lightly.)*

Thank you.

D'ARTAGNAN. I would do it again a thousand times, times another thousand and again after that. Order me to the Antipodes and I will be there by the end of the week.

CONSTANCE. I order you to wait on me tomorrow at the palace when I will have more time.

D'ARTAGNAN. It shall be done. Good night, my darling.

> *(They kiss beautifully.)*

D'ARTAGNAN. Good night.

CONSTANCE. Good night.

SEPTIME. Good night.

> *(***CONSTANCE** *and* **SEPTIME** *go.* **D'ARTAGNAN** *is alone and twirls around happily.)*

I am in love! Ha haaaaaaa! Do you hear that Paris! I Am In Love!

(At which moment **ROCHEFORT** *comes out of the shadows and smashes* **D'ARTAGNAN** *on the head, knocking him out.)*

ROCHEFORT. I'm in love too, but I don't make a spectacle of myself.

(He drags **D'ARTAGNAN** *away.)*

Scene Ten

(A room in the cardinal's palace, the next morning. The **KING**, **TREVILLE**, *and the* **CARDINAL***, who is enraged.)*

CARDINAL RICHELIEU. *Sire, I find it unforgivable!*

KING LOUIS. The facts, Your Eminence. I need the facts. Treville, tell me again. You say that the *cardinal's* guards were beaten by *my* musketeers last night behind the Luxembourg.

TREVILLE. That's correct, Your Majesty. In fact, your musketeers were badly outnumbered.

KING LOUIS. *(To the* **CARDINAL***.)* Oh my dear fellow, I'm so sorry. I feel awful about it.

(Then he bursts into laughter.)

Bwa ha ha ha ha ha ha ha ha ha ha!

CARDINAL RICHELIEU. The men are criminals, Sire! They should be punished!

KING LOUIS. Yes, yes, I agree, absolutely.

TREVILLE. Punished.

KING LOUIS. Arrested.

TREVILLE. Disciplined.

KING LOUIS. Strongly.

KING LOUIS & TREVILLE. …Bwa ha ha ha ha ha ha ha ha ha!

(They exit, their laughter ringing through the halls. The **CARDINAL** *is furious.* **ROCHEFORT** *enters.)*

ROCHEFORT. Your Grace, I have something to report.

CARDINAL RICHELIEU. Oh really?

ROCHEFORT. Yes, your Grace, there's been a development *AAAAARRRGGGHHH!*

(The **CARDINAL** *is strangling him again. Really going at it this time.)*

CARDINAL RICHELIEU. Development?! There's a *DEVELOPMENT?!*

ROCHEFORT. Argh... Argh...please... I've got him...the boy. D'Artagnan. He's right outside!

(*The* **CARDINAL** *drops* **ROCHEFORT**, *who gasps for air.*)

CARDINAL RICHELIEU. Really?

ROCHEFORT. He says he doesn't know anything.

CARDINAL RICHELIEU. Bring him. Now!

ROCHEFORT. Yes, Your Eminence.

(**ROCHEFORT** *exits, then brings* **D'ARTAGNAN** *into the room, dragging him shackled.* **D'ARTAGNAN** *has been beaten, and he falls to his knees.*)

CARDINAL RICHELIEU. Ah. Welcome, young man, to my humble abode.

(**D'ARTAGNAN** *tries to get up, but* **ROCHEFORT** *pushes him down.*)

ROCHEFORT. Down, dog! And say thank you!

CARDINAL RICHELIEU. Rochefort, Rochefort. Not so rough. I'm sure this young man wants to cooperate. Now what's your name again?

D'ARTAGNAN. D'Artagnan.

CARDINAL RICHELIEU. Ah yes, of course. D'Artagnan. Now you know, of course, who *I* am, and you know that I have a job to do, and that my job requires information. Now tell me who hired you to rescue Constance Bonacieux.

D'ARTAGNAN. No one, Your Grace. I just happened to meet her.

(*Wham!* **ROCHEFORT** *hits him violently on the back again.*)

CARDINAL RICHELIEU. Wrong answer. Let's try it again. Who hired you?

D'ARTAGNAN. Your Grace, it's the truth.

(*Wham! Same thing.*)

CARDINAL RICHELIEU. You're just not getting the hang of this. Let's try another question. Athos, Porthos and Aramis. I understand they're friends of yours. Oh, don't look so surprised. I know everything. Now, the fact is, I'd like to speak with them, and I need their address. Do you know it?

D'ARTAGNAN. Go to hell.

> *(Wham!)*

CARDINAL RICHELIEU. All right, just kill him. Do it now. Instantly.

> **(ROCHEFORT** *pulls out a dagger and grabs* **D'ARTAGNAN** *by the hair.)*

Wait. On second thought, he might be useful. Chain him up and come with me. Make sure that he isn't comfortable.

> *(The* **CARDINAL** *exits, and* **ROCHEFORT** *chains* **D'ARTAGNAN** *to the wall.)*

ROCHEFORT. You little upstart. Just wait'll he says the word. You're as good as dead.

> **(ROCHEFORT** *gives him a last punch and exits in the direction of the cardinal.* **D'ARTAGNAN** *is alone and tries desperately to release himself – at which moment* **SOPHIE DELACROIX** *enters the room. She's a young woman, perhaps twenty. She has her hair pulled back and is dressed modestly. She's frightened of life – and when she sees* **D'ARTAGNAN**, *her mouth hangs open in complete wonder.)*

SOPHIE. Are you "D'Artagnan"?

D'ARTAGNAN. Yes.

SOPHIE. I overheard just now. I was listening.
(Referring to his wounds.) I-I had no idea...

D'ARTAGNAN. Who are you?

SOPHIE. I'm Sophie. Delacroix. The cardinal is my uncle.

D'ARTAGNAN. Your uncle?

SOPHIE. But why is he doing this to you? What have you done wrong?

D'ARTAGNAN. I've done nothing wrong! I promise you. He thinks I know something but I don't. I swear to you! You see, I-I bumped into this woman, literally, on the street, and she was in trouble and I helped her out and that's all I know!

SOPHIE. Everyone says that my uncle is unkind. But I don't think so. I-I love my uncle.

D'ARTAGNAN. I'm sure you do. A-and he must think I know something. But I really don't, and now he's going to kill me.

SOPHIE. He wouldn't do that.

D'ARTAGNAN. He said so! Just a minute ago! Could you help me? Please.

> *(She thinks a moment – then starts pulling at the chains around his wrists.)*

You're very kind. If you can somehow open the lock...

SOPHIE. It's very hard. I can't quite...

D'ARTAGNAN. Please hurry!

SOPHIE. Wait!

> *(She hurries to the desk and grabs a letter opener, then tries to use it to get into the lock.)*

Here! If I could just...somehow...

> *(Suddenly, we hear a noise from outside the room.)*

Shh! I hear something.

> *(At which moment she drops the opener on the floor.)*

Oh drat drat drat!

> *(And now we hear the **CARDINAL**'s voice outside the door:)*

CARDINAL RICHELIEU. *(Offstage.)* Won't be a moment!

D'ARTAGNAN. He's coming back!

SOPHIE. Oh no!

> *(She searches for the opener, finds it, and puts it back on the desk.)*

D'ARTAGNAN. Listen to me. I have a sister named Sabine and she's starting school today at the Convent of the Sacred Heart on the Rue Bourget.

> *(**SOPHIE** is staring at the door in terror.)*

Are you listening?!

SOPHIE. Yes!

D'ARTAGNAN. If you could go there now and tell her I'm in trouble, she'll know how to get to my friends and they'll try to help me. All right?

SOPHIE. Your sister. Convent of the Sacred Heart. Rue Bourget.

D'ARTAGNAN. God bless you.

> *(The door starts to open, and **SOPHIE** gasps and springs away from **D'ARTAGNAN**. The **CARDINAL** enters with **ROCHEFORT**. Meanwhile, **D'ARTAGNAN** lies still, pretending to be unconscious.)*

CARDINAL RICHELIEU. My dear. What are you – when did you get here –

SOPHIE. I just arrived. I-I let myself in. I heard noises and I'm so confused. Is he (dead)...

CARDINAL RICHELIEU. Oh, he'll recover beautifully. Rochefort.

ROCHEFORT. Yes, Your Grace.

CARDINAL RICHELIEU. Monsieur D'Artagnan needs your assistance. Take him away and keep him safe. My niece is concerned for his well-being.

> *(**ROCHEFORT** grabs **D'ARTAGNAN** and roughly yanks him to his feet, making **SOPHIE** gasp. He hauls **D'ARTAGNAN** out of the room, closing the door behind them.)*

Don't worry, my dear. He'll be well taken care of.

SOPHIE. Good. You know what they say: Waste not, want not.

> (**SOPHIE** *pulls off her wig and stands up straight. It's* **MILADY**.)

And we wouldn't want to waste a boy like that.

CARDINAL RICHELIEU. Ha ha! Well done, well done. Now what did he say?

MILADY. He said he has a sister – in school no less. She knows where to find the musketeers, and I suspect that she knows more than that. He gave me the address and begged me to go see her.

CARDINAL RICHELIEU. He begged you to go see her. My God, you're a genius.

MILADY. I only learn form the best, Your Eminence. Personally, I think you're wasted as a cardinal. You should be the pope.

CARDINAL RICHELIEU. You know I suggested that to Rome once, but it turns out I have too many children. Now off you go, it's time for school and I believe you have a young friend to visit? Here. You might find these useful.

> (*He hands* **MILADY** *a set of rosary beads. We will see how lethal they are in the next scene.*)

MILADY. Shall I kill her when I'm finished with her?

CARDINAL RICHELIEU. I leave that entirely to your discretion. Bon Voyage.

> (*And the scene changes to:*)

Scene Eleven

(The courtyard of the cardinal's palace, immediately following. **ROCHEFORT** *is dragging* **D'ARTAGNAN** *across the stones. They pass in front of* **THREE BEGGARS**, *pathetic creatures, products of the cardinal's cruelty.)*

ROCHEFORT. Come along, pretty-boy. Stop dragging your feet.

RAVANCHE. *(Entering.)* What's goin' on?

ROCHEFORT. Cardinal's orders. They're going after his sister for the information.

D'ARTAGNAN. My sister?

(Wham! **ROCHEFORT** *hits him in the head.)*

ROCHEFORT. The cardinal said we're to kill him.

RAVANCHE. Now?

(During the following speech, the **THREE BEGGARS** *rise up behind the two villains.)*

ROCHEFORT. Well let's see, I suppose we could toy with him for awhile first, like them villains do in the story books, thereby giving him time to come up with a plan of escape while some of his friends appear out of nowhere and cut the villains to pieces NOW WHAT DO YOU THINK?!

RAVANCHE. Right. Let's do it.

*(***RAVANCHE** *pulls his sword, but just as he's about to run* **D'ARTAGNAN** *through, a sword appears form under the cloak of one of the* **BEGGARS** *and parries him. Then all the* **BEGGARS** *throw off their cloaks, and we see that they're the* **MUSKETEERS**.*)*

ROCHEFORT. *(To* **RAVANCHE**.*)* I'll be right back!

*(***ROCHEFORT** *runs away. With a flick of his wrist,* **ATHOS** *skewers* **RAVANCHE**, *who drops to the ground.)*

D'ARTAGNAN. We have to get to Sabine right away!
PORTHOS. We heard!
ARAMIS. Let's go!
ATHOS. This way!

> *(As they go, we hear the voices of school girls singing a French song of the period.* Simultaneously, the scene changes to:)*

---

*A license to produce *The Three Musketeers* does not include a performance license for any third-party or copyrighted music. Licensees should create an original composition or use music in the public domain. For further information, please see Music Use Note on page 3.

Scene Twelve

(The Convent of the Sacred Heart. A few minutes later. As the lights come up, the MOTHER SUPERIOR *enters with* SABINE.*)*

MOTHER SUPERIOR. And this is where you'll begin your studies, along with the other girls.

SABINE. It's beautiful.

(A SISTER *enters, followed by* MILADY.*)*

SISTER. Excuse me, Mother. Miss Sabine has a visitor. Miss Sophie Delacroix, the cardinal's niece.

*(*MILADY *enters, dressed once again as* SOPHIE.*)*

MOTHER SUPERIOR. How do you do.

MILADY. How do you do, Mother. You must be Sabine.

SABINE. I am.

MILADY. I-I need to speak with you. I have a message from your brother.

(To MOTHER SUPERIOR.*)* Do you mind?

MOTHER SUPERIOR. Of course not. Take your time.

*(*MOTHER SUPERIOR *and the* SISTER *leave.)*

SABINE. From my brother?

MILADY. Yes! I-I'm afraid he's in terrible trouble. He's a prisoner of my uncle, Cardinal Richelieu.

SABINE. What?!

MILADY. Believe me, I-I know all about my uncle's ways, and I've tried to ignore it, but when I saw your brother this morning being tortured –

SABINE. Tortured? Oh my God! Is he –?

MILADY. He'll live. If we can get to my uncle in time with the information.

SABINE. What information?

MILADY. About Constance Bonacieux.

SABINE. That's the woman whose life he saved.

MILADY. Exactly. And apparently your brother had some ties to her before yesterday. He knew where she'd be. He was sent to save her.

SABINE. No, I don't think so.

MILADY. Yes, he was, and you must tell me the truth! They talked about killing him this afternoon!

SABINE. Oh Lord God! I-I-I don't know. He said he met her on the street by accident.

MILADY. But he knew who she was!

SABINE. Wait. He said if I needed anything I should talk to Athos.

MILADY. The musketeer?

SABINE. Yes. And his two friends, Porthos and Aramis.

MILADY. Good, good. Do you know where to find them?

SABINE. Yes. Come with me, I'll take you there.

MILADY. But what's the address? In case we somehow get separated. It will be safer, I promise.

SABINE. Forty-two Rue des Anges. That's where they live.

MILADY. The three of them? Will they be there now?

SABINE. Yes, I would think so. Oh please come on! We're wasting time!

MILADY. Wait. We must pray first. Look at these. Aren't they beautiful?

SABINE. They're rosary beads.

MILADY. That's what they look like, but they're much, much stronger. You can pull them as hard as you like and they won't break. Feel.

> (*Suddenly,* **MILADY** *whips the beads around* **SABINE***'s throat and starts to garrote her.* **SABINE** *fights back, desperately trying to get her fingers between the beads and her neck. At which moment the* **MOTHER SUPERIOR** *re-enters.*)

MOTHER SUPERIOR. My dear, it's about time we... What's happening? Stop it! What are you doing?! Help! Someone help!

MILADY. *Be quiet!*

> (**MILADY** *throws* **SABINE** *to the ground, then rushes over to the* **MOTHER SUPERIOR** *and stabs her in the gut.*)

VOICES. *(Offstage.)* Through here! This way! I think I see them!

MILADY. Oh, drat, drat, drat.

> (**MILADY** *runs out. At which moment the* **MUSKETEERS** *and* **D'ARTAGNAN** *run into the room.*)

D'ARTAGNAN. Sabine!

> *(He takes her in his arms.)*

Sabine! Oh, Sabine, say something! *Sabine, please!*

> *(Is she alive? Then:)*

SABINE. I'm... I'm...

D'ARTAGNAN. She's alive!

ARAMIS. Oh thank God.

ATHOS. You know what this means, don't you?

> *(As each one speaks, he draws his sword:)*

War on the cardinal.

ARAMIS. War on the cardinal.

PORTHOS. War on the cardinal.

THREE MUSKETEERS. All for one.

SABINE. *(Weakly, from the ground.)* And one for all.

> *(Blackout.)*

End of Act One

ACT II

Scene One

(Act Two opens with a montage set to music. * *It tells the story of what happens between the acts. It opens with* **D'ARTAGNAN** *and the* **MUSKETEERS** *with their swords crossed.)*

ALL. War on the cardinal!

(Lush, romantic music swells up * *as the four men run off in different directions. This reveals the* **KING**, *tending his bees. He's wearing a 17th century beekeeping outfit and he uses a 17th century spraying device to keep the bees in line. He remains center stage as the following action swirls about him:)*

(First, we see the **MUSKETEERS** *and the cardinal's* **GUARDS** *fighting around the* **KING**, *who remains oblivious. Then we see the* **DUKE OF BUCKINGHAM** *for the first time. Secretly he meets the* **QUEEN**, *and they embrace. She tells him that they must part forever, and the* **DUKE** *protests. He tries to kiss her and she resists – no more! Meanwhile,* **MILADY** *goes by and observes them, then heads for the* **CARDINAL**.)*

(Meanwhile, **SABINE** *pursues* **ARAMIS**, *who keeps dodging her. Then* **D'ARTAGNAN** *and*

---

*A license to produce *The Three Musketeers* does not include a performance license for any third-party or copyrighted music. Licensees should create an original composition or use music in the public domain. For further information, please see Music Use Note on page 3.

CONSTANCE *are seen embracing. The* QUEEN *then hurries up to* CONSTANCE *and interrupts to give her instructions.* CONSTANCE *hurries off.)*

*(*ATHOS *and* ROCHEFORT *pass by, dueling – then* PORTHOS *against three* GUARDS *at once – as* CONSTANCE *returns with a box, and inside the box is the Valmont necklace, a distinctive piece of jewelry with twelve large diamonds set in gold. The* QUEEN *takes it to* BUCKINGHAM *as a parting gift. He protests and tries to kiss her again, but she resists and sends him away with the necklace. Meanwhile, the* KING *continues spraying his bees and remains clueless.)*

(Now we see MILADY *joining the* CARDINAL *to tell him the news: they have leverage with the queen and must use it. In a final swirl of activity, the montage ends as the* CARDINAL *tells the* KING *about the affair and the necklace.)*

KING LOUIS. Unbelievable! It's unbelievable! My own darling wife carrying on with some-some-some duke or other?

CARDINAL RICHELIEU. The Duke of Buckingham.

KING LOUIS. She could be hanged for that!

CARDINAL RICHELIEU. The queen, Sire?

KING LOUIS. And the man's from England. I mean, he's-he's-he's-he's English. They're all so polite. It's amazing they have any children at all.

CARDINAL RICHELIEU. Perhaps it isn't true, Your Highness.

KING LOUIS. Of course it's true. I heard it from one of your own people!

CARDINAL RICHELIEU. And he told you about the necklace, I presume.

KING LOUIS. Necklace? What necklace?

CARDINAL RICHELIEU. The Valmont necklace. The one she gave to the Duke of Buckingham as a present before he went back to England.

KING LOUIS. *(Thunderstruck.)* She gave the duke the Valmont necklace?

CARDINAL RICHELIEU. Oh, dear. I shouldn't have said that.

KING LOUIS. I gave that to her as a wedding gift. It has twelve diamonds in it. They're as big as chicken eggs!

CARDINAL RICHELIEU. Of course we don't have any proof she gave it to him.

KING LOUIS. Oh I'll get proof, don't you worry. I'll have her searched! I'll have her rooms searched! Ow!

    (A bee sting.)

CARDINAL RICHELIEU. Sire, you can't do that. She's the Queen of France. It could start a war.

KING LOUIS. With her horrible father you mean. The King of Austria. She should have stayed in Austria with all that yodeling.

CARDINAL RICHELIEU. That's Switzerland, Sire.

KING LOUIS. Austria, Switzerland. The point is, we need proof and there's no way to get it.

CARDINAL RICHELIEU. Yes. Except…no.

KING LOUIS. What?

CARDINAL RICHELIEU. Oh, it wouldn't work.

KING LOUIS. What is it? Tell me.

CARDINAL RICHELIEU. You could give a ball.

KING LOUIS. A ball?

CARDINAL RICHELIEU. For some important occasion that might be occurring in the next week or so.

KING LOUIS. My birthday's next week. We could use that.

CARDINAL RICHELIEU. Oh what a good idea, Sire. I never thought of that.

KING LOUIS. But why a ball?

CARDINAL RICHELIEU. Well, you could tell the queen that she had to wear the necklace at the ball. No one could object to that.

KING LOUIS. And then, if she refused to wear it, we'd have the proof!

CARDINAL RICHELIEU. That's brilliant, Sire.

KING LOUIS. But what if this awful duke fellow gives the necklace back?

CARDINAL RICHELIEU. He's in England, Sire, and your birthday is Monday. It's three hundred miles.

KING LOUIS. So it is. I see. Ha ha! Of course! Oh balls, balls, I love balls! I'll start planning the menu right away. But what if I catch her? I'd have to send her home. Ugh. Let's not think about that. Come with me. There's so much to do. Oh this is marvelous!

> *(As soon as they're gone, **CONSTANCE** appears from behind a screen. She's heard everything. She dashes out and into the queen's chamber, where the **QUEEN** sits reading a letter.)*

CONSTANCE. Your Highness! Your Highness!

QUEEN ANNE. Constance, what is it?

CONSTANCE. Oh Your Highness, I have some bad news.

QUEEN ANNE. *(Her hand to her throat.)* He knows.

CONSTANCE. Yes.

QUEEN ANNE. Oh, what'll I do?! He'll call it treason!

CONSTANCE. We have to send someone to England right away to bring it back.

QUEEN ANNE. But no one could make the journey in time. Could they?

CONSTANCE. I think it's possible. Just. If we're lucky. And I've brought someone here. His name's D'Artagnan.

QUEEN ANNE. Your young man from Gascony?

CONSTANCE. Yes. I'd trust him with my life.

QUEEN ANNE. Bring him in. Please.

> *(**CONSTANCE** goes out and comes back with **D'ARTAGNAN**.)*

D'ARTAGNAN. Your Majesty.

QUEEN ANNE. Monsieur D'Artagnan. I-I've done something foolish. Do you think you can help me?

D'ARTAGNAN. I can try, madam.

QUEEN ANNE. I must warn you: this whole affair is vital to the cardinal. If I'm exposed, he'll use it to undermine the king's authority and try to seize power for himself.

D'ARTAGNAN. I understand. But may I ask a favor?

QUEEN ANNE. Anything.

D'ARTAGNAN. I have three friends who would like to go with me, and I believe them vital to the mission. Their names are Athos, Porthos –

QUEEN ANNE. And Aramis. The three inseparables. Of course you can take them. I'll be grateful for their help. But let me hurry now and write a letter you can show the duke. And please: be careful.

> (*The* **QUEEN** *rushes out* – **D'ARTAGNAN** *and* **CONSTANCE** *embrace as scene changes to:*)

Scene Two

(The cardinal's palace. An angry **CARDINAL**
confers with **MILADY**.*)*

MILADY. But Your Eminence, it's three hundred miles. That's impossible.

CARDINAL RICHELIEU. It is not impossible. I have just received word that Athos, Porthos and Aramis – along with that vomitous little rat D'Artagnan – are setting out for England as we speak. You must get to England before they do and find Buckingham and get the necklace at any cost.

MILADY. You know he isn't going to just hand it over.

CARDINAL RICHELIEU. And why do you think I'm sending you? He's a man, isn't he? Isn't that your stock in trade?

MILADY. *(Stiffens; this is offensive to her.)* Yes. Of course it is.

CARDINAL RICHELIEU. Now when you find him, I want you to pry two of the diamonds out of the necklace and get them back here as fast as you can.

MILADY. Why not the whole necklace?

CARDINAL RICHELIEU. Because the queen has half of France looking for the "whole necklace." You'll be stopped at the border on your way back and searched thoroughly. But surely you can hide two diamonds from the customs officers – even if they are as big as chickens' eggs. The diamonds, not –

CARDINAL RICHELIEU & MILADY. The customs officers.

CARDINAL RICHELIEU. Can we please stop talking now so you can find a horse or a chaise or whatever you like and get on the road *and get to England.* Just for once I'd like to beat those revolting do-gooders at their own game.

MILADY. Yes, Sire. Without delay.

(She hurries off. Immediately we hear cries of preparation and we're into:)

Scene Three

(Various locations. Our four heroes – **ATHOS**, **ARAMIS**, **PORTHOS**, *and* **D'ARTAGNAN** *– appear, buckling their swords on.)*

ATHOS. Gentlemen, there's no time to lose.

PORTHOS. Hurry, racing, always racing. Whatever happened to civility, eh? And a fair fight?

ARAMIS. The queen's reputation is what happened, Porthos. She'll lose it if we don't hurry.

PORTHOS. Well she shouldn't have misplaced it, if you ask me.

ATHOS. Gentlemen, listen. I propose a rule for our journey. If any of us falls along the way, the others continue without him. Agreed?

PORTHOS, ARAMIS & D'ARTAGNAN. Agreed.

(The **CARDINAL** *and* **ROCHEFORT** *appear on a balcony above the action. Their conversation occurs simultaneously with our heroes' journey and covers the same time frame.)*

CARDINAL RICHELIEU. Rochefort.

ROCHEFORT. Sire.

CARDINAL RICHELIEU. Would you cease shilly-shallying and tell me, did your men stop the musketeers or not?!

ROCHEFORT. I-I don't think so, Sire. Not yet.

CARDINAL RICHELIEU. That's unacceptable. What happened at Louvier? Did you do as I instructed?

ROCHEFORT. To the letter, Your Eminence. The innkeeper there was a great supporter of yours.

CARDINAL RICHELIEU. "Was"?

(We're now at the Inn at Louvier. A weasel-like **INNKEEPER** *is speaking to the* **MUSKETEERS**, *who are pulling their hats off and catching their breaths.)*

INNKEEPER. A glass of wine, gentlemen?

PORTHOS. Yes, yes, to be sure.

ARAMIS. I'm willing to bet this mission's going to be more dangerous than we thought.

PORTHOS. *(To the* **INNKEEPER**.*)* How much for the wine?

INNKEEPER. It has been paid for by your young friend outside.

ATHOS. Good lad.

PORTHOS. We'll drink his health.

> *(The* **INNKEEPER** *begins pouring.)*

ARAMIS. Or the health of his mistress who got us into this mess.

PORTHOS. To Constance! For being a minx.

ARAMIS & ATHOS. To Constance!

> *(The* **MUSKETEERS** *are about to drink when* **D'ARTAGNAN** *enters – the* **INNKEEPER** *is startled to see him.)*

D'ARTAGNAN. What's that about Constance?

PORTHOS. Oh nothing, nothing.

INNKEEPER. Uh, sir – what about the horses? You should go tend to them.

D'ARTAGNAN. They're taken care of.

INNKEEPER. But they need to be fed, and-and-and watered. I mean, the shape they're in, they...

D'ARTAGNAN. I said they're taken care of.

ATHOS. Your health, my boy.

ARAMIS. With thanks for the bottle. It was very generous.

PORTHOS. Though I doubt if it's much of a vintage at a place like this.

> *(***PORTHOS** *is about to put his tankard to his lips when* **D'ARTAGNAN** *knocks it away.)*

D'ARTAGNAN. *Wait!*

> *(The tankard clatters onto the floor.)*

PORTHOS. Are you mad?!

D'ARTAGNAN. I didn't send you a bottle. Who told you I did?

ARAMIS. This fellow here.

INNKEEPER. I-I must have been confused.

D'ARTAGNAN. Perhaps you'll taste it for us.

INNKEEPER. I-I don't drink, sir. I-I-I mean I'm not thirsty.

D'ARTAGNAN. Well you'll drink this bottle, do you hear?! Now drink it down!

INNKEEPER. No!

D'ARTAGNAN. *Drink it!*

> (**D'ARTAGNAN** *forces the* **INNKEEPER** *to drink the wine. The man swallows...and to everyone's surprise, the drink has no effect. The* **INNKEEPER** *smiles happily and the others raise their tankards again.*)

THREE MUSKETEERS & D'ARTAGNAN. To Constance!

> (*The* **INNKEEPER** *coughs. Beat. Everyone thinks a moment, then shrugs.*)

To Constance!

> (*Cough, cough. The* **MUSKETEERS** *get it now. The* **INNKEEPER** *turns pale, coughs some more, doubles over in pain, and then has the most hideous fit one has ever seen as the poison runs its lethal course. By the end, he is foaming at the mouth and lies dead on the floor.*)

PORTHOS. Damn waste. It smelled rather good.

> (*We now see the* **CARDINAL** *and* **ROCHEFORT** *again.*)

CARDINAL RICHELIEU. Well in that case what happened at Beauvais?

ROCHEFORT. I'm afraid there were difficulties, Your Grace.

CARDINAL RICHELIEU. But I thought you had them outnumbered.

ROCHEFORT. I believe that the musketeers, having a noble cause to fight for – one that is pure and true – have somehow acquired an inner strength, as though God himself has summoned them to fight for –

CARDINAL RICHELIEU. Oh shut up.

> *(We're now at an outdoor tavern at Beauvais. Our heroes have just arrived and dismounted, and a stranger named **FACHE** is raising his flagon of wine, backed up by a number of his belligerent cohorts.)*

FACHE. You there! In the fancy dress! I propose a toast!

PORTHOS. Me, sir?

FACHE. To the leader of France: His Eminence, Cardinal Richelieu!

PORTHOS. I believe you're mistaken, sir. Our toast is to the king.

FACHE. To the cardinal I say!

PORTHOS. I say the king.

FACHE. Then I say may you go to hell!

PORTHOS. *(Pulling his sword and twirling it expertly.)* You go first. I'll follow if it looks pleasant.

ARAMIS. Look! It's a trap! There's more of them!

PORTHOS. No! No! Stay back. I'll hold them off. You go on as we agreed.

ATHOS. But it's five to one.

PORTHOS. Yes, I know. The question is, do I let any of them live? Go on, go on. Just get out of here!

> *(***PORTHOS*** *battles on – as we shift our focus back to the* **CARDINAL** *and* **ROCHEFORT**:*)*

CARDINAL RICHELIEU. So then at Calais you used road workers?

ROCHEFORT. That's right, Your Eminence.

CARDINAL RICHELIEU. Why in the name of heaven would you use road workers to attack musketeers?

ROCHEFORT. It was part of the plan, Your Grace. They weren't really road workers. They were disguised that way in order to catch the musketeers off-guard.

CARDINAL RICHELIEU. Well, that's not a terrible plan.

ROCHEFORT. It was an excellent plan, Sire.

CARDINAL RICHELIEU. And did it work?

ROCHEFORT. No.

> (*And we're back with the* **MUSKETEERS**, *who are tramping along a narrow, muddy road.*)

ARAMIS. Damn their eyes, just look what's happening to these new boots. Can't they finish the road…

ATHOS. Aramis –

ARAMIS. They should leave a pathway so that boots like this don't get ruined!

ATHOS. Aramis –

ARAMIS. These were brand new when I left Paris –

ATHOS. Aramis forget the boots!

ARAMIS. Why is that?

> (*Bang! Muskets are fired from offstage. As bullets whiz by, our heroes jump for cover.*)

D'ARTAGNAN. It's an ambush!

ARAMIS. Look out!

ATHOS. Take cover!

> (*Bang!* **ARAMIS** *is wounded in the leg.* **D'ARTAGNAN** *drags him to safety.*)

ARAMIS. Damn their eyes, we'd be safer at the Siege of La Rochelle!

> (**ATHOS** *pulls a pistol.*)

ATHOS. D'Artagnan, go. I'll see to Aramis.

ARAMIS. See to me? That's ridiculous! It's only a little Ah!

ATHOS. Would you please go!

D'ARTAGNAN. But there's at least eight of them!

> (*Bang!* **ATHOS** *shoots one.*)

ATHOS. Now there's seven.

> (**D'ARTAGNAN** *hesitates.*)

ATHOS. Go! Quickly! It's your duty, man! Just watch your
back! Now go, go, go!

(**D'ARTAGNAN** *makes a dash for it as we go to:*)

Scene Four

(London. The palace of the Duke of Buckingham. A day later. We see **MILADY** *rushing away from the palace, tossing two diamonds happily in her hands. Then we see the* **DUKE OF BUCKINGHAM** *at his mirror, shaving. Standing nearby is his punctilious major-domo,* **STANLEY**.*)*

STANLEY. Sir. May I present Monsieur D'Artagnan? He's from Paris, sir.

BUCKINGHAM. I'm the Duke of Buckingham and you want me to meet some French peasant?

STANLEY. He does seem to be an upstart, sir. But he has brought a letter from the Queen of France.

BUCKINGHAM. Let me see that.

(He scans the letter.)

Send him in. And bring me the necklace.

*(***STANLEY*** exits, then* **D'ARTAGNAN** *enters, out of breath.)*

D'ARTAGNAN. Your Grace.

BUCKINGHAM. Monsieur D'Artagnan. I see here that you're a friend to Queen Anne.

D'ARTAGNAN. I have that honor, sir.

BUCKINGHAM. It says there's to be a ball next week.

D'ARTAGNAN. That's correct, Your Grace.

BUCKINGHAM. And you know about the necklace, apparently.

D'ARTAGNAN. I'm afraid I do, sir. And I'm ready to ride back with it immediately.

BUCKINGHAM. You're a brave fellow and I'm in your debt. Here it is.

*(***STANLEY*** enters, carrying a jewel box. The* **DUKE** *takes it and opens it.)*

As you can see, it's extremely valuable –

D'ARTAGNAN. Excuse me, sir, but aren't there meant to be twelve diamonds?

BUCKINGHAM. That's right. There are twelve. Count them.

D'ARTAGNAN. I have, sir, and there are only ten.

BUCKINGHAM. Let me see that. Of course there are tw– ... Good Lord! That's impossible! This has been locked up ever since Anne gave it to me.

D'ARTAGNAN. Are you certain, Your Grace?

BUCKINGHAM. Of course I'm certain. It's been in my vault. The only time –

D'ARTAGNAN. The only time what, sir?

BUCKINGHAM. The only time it wasn't locked up was last night. I...showed it to this woman. I don't know why. I just did. She flattered me.

D'ARTAGNAN. Do you know her name, sir?

BUCKINGHAM. The Countess de Winter. I-I met her at a party. She came back here and...for a short time she was in my bedroom – alone with the necklace. She must have removed two of the diamonds. The witch!

D'ARTAGNAN. Sir, do you know where she is?

BUCKINGHAM. She said she was going back to Paris this morning. Back to –

BUCKINGHAM & D'ARTAGNAN. The cardinal.

BUCKINGHAM. When is the ball?

D'ARTAGNAN. On Monday.

BUCKINGHAM. I'll close all the ports on some pretext in case she hasn't crossed the Channel yet. Stanley!

STANLEY. Sir.

BUCKINGHAM. Fetch my jeweler. Bring him here this minute.

D'ARTAGNAN. Your jeweler?

BUCKINGHAM. The diamonds match. I'll have him cut two more and insert them into the setting. You shouldn't have to wait more than a day. In the meantime, I'll post ahead and arrange fresh horses for you, a new mount every twenty miles.

D'ARTAGNAN. I'll do my best, sir, but...what if I'm too late?
BUCKINGHAM. Then the queen is lost.

    (Music strikes up*, and we're at:)

---

*A license to produce *The Three Musketeers* does not include a performance license for any third-party or copyrighted music. Licensees should create an original composition or use music in the public domain. For further information, please see Music Use Note on page 3.

Scene Five

(The royal ball. Everything is splendid. An orchestra is playing, and all the guests, including the **MUSKETEERS***, wear masks representing different animals. After a moment the* **CARDINAL** *appears as a stag. Then* **ROCHEFORT** *enters, his mask a dog with a black nose and floppy ears.)*

CARDINAL RICHELIEU. Rochefort?

ROCHEFORT. Your Eminence.

CARDINAL RICHELIEU. What are you wearing?

ROCHEFORT. I'm a dog, Sire.

CARDINAL RICHELIEU. I thought you were coming as a beaver.

ROCHEFORT. I was, but the teeth were killing me.

CARDINAL RICHELIEU. Has Milady arrived yet?

ROCHEFORT. It's hard to tell, Your Grace. Is she a mammal?

CARDINAL RICHELIEU. How should I know, you idiot. I just want the diamonds. She was due back from London this morning.

> *(Angry.)*

Yes?!

> *(This last to* **MILADY***, who has come up from behind and tapped him on the shoulder. She is masked as a hawk and looks dangerous and attractive.)*

MILADY. Machiavelli once said that if you can't enjoy a party, then just don't go.

CARDINAL RICHELIEU. There you are. It's about time.

MILADY. I just rode three hundred miles in four days on a very hard saddle with a brief stopover in a certain bedroom, so I wouldn't be too impatient if I were you.

CARDINAL RICHELIEU. Did you obtain the diamonds?

> *(***MILADY*** pulls out a box and opens it for him.)*

Oh, admirable. Well done. I'll pay you handsomely for this. Indeed, I may throw in a front-row seat at a certain Royal Hanging.

(The **KING** *enters wearing the mask and robes of a lion, with* **TREVILLE**, *who wears the mask of a panther.)*

KING LOUIS. Balls! Balls! I love balls! The dancing and the dresses and Ha! Balls!

CARDINAL RICHELIEU. Good evening, Your Majesty. I failed to notice if the queen has made her entrance yet.

KING LOUIS. No she hasn't, but I can't wait. I plan to examine her neck very carefully. Oh Lord. Who is that stunning creature over there? She looks scrumptious.

(He's looking at **SABINE**, *who has just entered. She's dressed as a peacock and looks very glamorous and grown-up indeed.)*

CARDINAL RICHELIEU. I have no idea, Your Highness.

KING LOUIS. I'll go make inquiries. Ha! Oh God, I love being King.

(As the **KING** *scurries away the music changes, and* **SABINE** *spots* **ARAMIS** *and goes up to him.)*

SABINE. *(Using a Slavic accent.)* Exoose me plis, and pardon me for interrupt like zees, but iss your name Meesyour Aramees, de musketeer?

ARAMIS. Yes, it is.

(They dance.)

Are you the Countess de Vergenne? You are, aren't you? I can tell from your perfume.

SABINE. Non.

ARAMIS. Wait. I know. La Duchesse de Martine?

SABINE. Non. You are wrohng agayn, my friend.

ARAMIS. Well I must say, whoever you are, you look stunning tonight, and I hope that you and I can become better – good God!

(**SABINE** *has flipped her mask aside so that he sees who it is.*)

ARAMIS. What are you doing here?!

SABINE. *(Delighted with herself.)* Are you surprised?

ARAMIS. Would you please just-just-just think of me as a brother!

SABINE. I already have a brother.

(**ARAMIS** *stomps his foot and walks away.*)

Wait! We haven't finished yet! And you're such a good dancer!

(**CONSTANCE** *enters and hurries up to* **SABINE**.)

CONSTANCE. Sabine!

SABINE. What's the matter?

CONSTANCE. It's D'Artagnan. No one's seen him yet!

SABINE. Well I wouldn't (worry) –

CONSTANCE. It was too much to hope – in four days. I only pray that nothing's happened to him.

(A fanfare sounds.)

Wait. Here comes the queen!

(**CONSTANCE** *hurries to the* **QUEEN**, *who is just entering in all her splendor. She wears the mask of an eagle. When she doffs her mask we see that she is not wearing the necklace.*)

KING LOUIS. What? What's this? No necklace?

CARDINAL RICHELIEU. Oh dear, oh dear.

(The **KING** *pushes his way across the room.)*

KING LOUIS. Excuse me. Excuse me. Madam, where is the necklace? Do you defy me? Do you humiliate me in front of my subjects?

QUEEN ANNE. Of course not, husband, I –

KING LOUIS. *(Enraged.)* Then where is it?! Are you hiding something from me? Is that your game?!

(Silence. Everyone at court is embarrassed.)

QUEEN ANNE. I-I was afraid to wear it, Sire. I thought it might get jostled in the crowd –

KING LOUIS. Oh, poppycock! That's ridiculous! It's-it's-it's unbelievable!

QUEEN ANNE. I-I'll have it fetched from the Louvre at once, Sire.

KING LOUIS. Please do so, Madam. The ballet starts in ten minutes. It's the "Merlaison." My favorite dance in the entire world. And I was intending to dance it with you!

> *(The **KING** moves away in a huff. The **QUEEN** wilts in defeat, and the guests shake their heads and murmur over the scene they've just witnessed.)*

QUEEN ANNE. *(To **CONSTANCE**.)* All is lost.

CONSTANCE. Not yet, Madam… *Wait! There he is!*

> *(At which moment we see **D'ARTAGNAN** rush into the room. Or perhaps he swings in, heroically.)*

Madam, he's here!

> *(**CONSTANCE** waves to him, and motions him to follow her and the **QUEEN** offstage.)*

Come with me, Your Majesty. Quickly. Quickly!

> *(She and the **QUEEN** exit, followed by **D'ARTAGNAN**. As they go, we refocus on the **KING** and the **CARDINAL**, who have seen none of this.)*

CARDINAL RICHELIEU. Your Highness, I believe there's something you should see.

> *(He pulls out the box and hands it to the **KING**.)*

KING LOUIS. What…what's the meaning of this? Two diamonds? They look exactly like the ones in the (necklace)!

CARDINAL RICHELIEU. If the queen does have the necklace, Sire, which I strongly doubt, I urge you to count the diamonds carefully. If she has only ten, you should ask her if she remembers how these two got away.

KING LOUIS. "Got away"? I-I-I... Wait! Look!

> *(The* **QUEEN** *re-enters. She is wearing the necklace. She takes the* **KING***'s hand and begins dancing with him. The* **KING***, determined to get to the bottom of all this, begins counting the diamonds. However, he can never quite finish the count and he keeps getting confused.)*

One, two, three, four, six...no five...oh, damn.

One, two, three, four, five...no, I counted that one.

One, two, three, four...

D'ARTAGNAN. *(To the* **MUSKETEERS***.)* My friends! How good to see you! I was afraid you'd be at La Rochelle by this time.

ATHOS. We go next month.

ARAMIS. Don't remind me.

PORTHOS. Unless you get us killed first on one of your harebrained errands.

SABINE. D'Artagnan! Did you bring back the necklace?

D'ARTAGNAN. I did. She's wearing it now.

KING LOUIS. Seven, six, seven...

SABINE. That's it? It doesn't look that impressive. It only has ten diamonds in it.

D'ARTAGNAN. No, it has twelve.

SABINE. No, ten. I have extremely good eyes.

D'ARTAGNAN. Sister, it's twelve. In fact, it had ten when I arrived in London, but then the duke himself had two more made, and I kept the whole necklace right here in my...

> *(***D'ARTAGNAN*** *pats the pockets of his cloak and feels something he doesn't expect. He looks bewildered. He thrusts his hand in his pocket and pulls out two large diamonds.)*

Oh no! They must have come loose during the journey!

KING LOUIS. Six, seven...

ATHOS. He's counting them.

SABINE. Oh, no!

ARAMIS. What'll we do?!

PORTHOS. Sabine, create a diversion.

SABINE. What?

PORTHOS. Do it now!

SABINE. But what'll I –? ...Wait, I've got an idea.

> *(She rushes to the middle of the room and pretends to faint.)*

Ohhhhhhhh!

GUESTS. Ah! What happened? / Is she all right? / Get her some salts!

> *(As the* **GUESTS** *react, we see the following deft maneuver:* **D'ARTAGNAN** *hands the two diamonds to* **ATHOS***, who hands them to* **ARAMIS***, who hands them to* **PORTHOS***, who hands them to* **CONSTANCE***, who hands them to the* **QUEEN***. This should be done with panache: thrown, perhaps, like juggling balls. When it's over, the* **KING** *is helping* **SABINE** *off the floor.)*

SABINE. I'm all right. Thank you. I must have fainted.

KING LOUIS. *(Taken with her beauty, trying to impress her.)* My dear young woman, I'll call my personal physician.

SABINE. There's no need really. It's just the baby. He always kicks up around this time.

> *(She pats her stomach and the* **KING** *backs off.)*

KING LOUIS. Just the...oh. Oh, I see!

SABINE. And look, here's the father! Oh Aramis, sweetheart. Isn't he handsome? I hope the baby looks just like him!

> *(She throws her arms around* **ARAMIS** *and he carries her away.)*

ARAMIS. Not. Funny.

KING LOUIS. Now let's see. Where was I? Oh yes. Of course. (*To the* **QUEEN**.) Stay still, Madam! One, two, three, four, five, six, seven, eight, nine, ten. Ten! Just as I thought.

QUEEN ANNE. Your Majesty –

KING LOUIS. I see that you have lost two of the diamonds, Madam. And look at this!

(*He pulls out the box and opens it.*)

QUEEN ANNE. You mean you're giving me two more? Louis, that makes fourteen!

KING LOUIS. Fourteen?

QUEEN ANNE. Yes. I have twelve already.

(*She holds out the two loose diamonds for him to see.*)

These two came out of their fittings as I was putting it on.

KING LOUIS. (*Confused.*) One two three four five six seven eight nine ten eleven twelve.

QUEEN ANNE. And now fourteen. How very kind.

KING LOUIS. …Richelieu. Richelieu! Is this a joke?

CARDINAL RICHELIEU. A joke, Your Highness? Of course not. It's more what I'd call a little game.

QUEEN ANNE. A game, Your Eminence. Oh, please tell us!

CARDINAL RICHELIEU. The fact is, I wanted to give Her Majesty a present of these two extra diamonds, but I didn't dare offer them myself, for reasons of protocol.

KING LOUIS. Protocol. Of course.

QUEEN ANNE. So then I have Your Eminence to thank for this generous gift. And yet they must have cost you even more dearly than the other twelve cost His Majesty.

CARDINAL RICHELIEU. They may have indeed, Your Highness. And yet I'm sure that next time, I shall come out even.

QUEEN ANNE. I will hold my breath. Oh, listen. It's the "Merlaison." Shall we, Louis?

(*She stretches out her hand to the* **KING**, *asking to dance.*)

KING LOUIS. Hm? Yes yes. Of course. The "Merlaison." Ha
ha! My Queen! Anne. How marvelous!

> *(As the **KING** turns to prepare for the dance,
> the **QUEEN** surreptitiously pulls a ring from
> her finger and hands it to **D'ARTAGNAN**,
> mouthing the words "Thank you.")*

> *(As she turns to join the **KING** for the dance we
> hear a loud explosion, and we're now in:)*

Scene Six

(Boom! It's the Siege of La Rochelle, and we're in a field with an abandoned farmhouse in the distance. Bullets are flying and we hear the voices of soldiers crying out in the distance. **TREVILLE, ATHOS, PORTHOS,** *and* **ARAMIS** *are in the middle of a skirmish, barricaded against their assailants. The* **MUSKETEERS** *are forced to shout to each other to be heard over the din of the muskets.)*

PORTHOS. *Tell me again?*

ARAMIS. *They're Protestants. They're called Huguenots. And they refuse to leave France.*

PORTHOS. *I can never keep these damn wars straight.*

ATHOS. *It's not a war. It's a siege.*

TREVILLE. *We talked about it. La Rochelle.*

PORTHOS. *Oh, right, right, right. The Catholics against the Protestants.*

ARAMIS. *Exactly.*

PORTHOS. *So you're telling me that Christians are killing each other over how much Latin they can use in church?*

ATHOS. *Stop asking sensible questions and keep your head down!*

　　　(Bang! Bang!)

TREVILLE. *Enough! You two circle 'round. Athos, make for that abandoned farmhouse there and cover our backs. I'm going for reinforcements.*

　　　(Bang! Bang! **ATHOS** *runs off in one direction,* **PORTHOS** *and* **ARAMIS** *in the other as* **TREVILLE** *exits.)*

Scene Seven

(The action shifts to the inside of the farmhouse, where we see the **CARDINAL** *and* **MILADY** *in discussion.)*

MILADY. Enough is enough! I say we kill her!

CARDINAL RICHELIEU. And I say no. I'm aware of exactly who needs killing at the moment and it isn't Constance Bonacieux.

MILADY. Who is it?

CARDINAL RICHELIEU. The king.

*(***MILADY*** reacts. This is a surprise, even for her.)*

The little toad refuses to go to war with England. He's even started peace negotiations over the siege. And he's doing it behind my back!

MILADY. It sounds like he's getting a mind of his own.

CARDINAL RICHELIEU. Well not for long. If the king is assassinated and the English are blamed, I think I can count on my little war, don't you?

MILADY. And then, of course, there's the question of who rules France if there's no clear heir to the throne.

CARDINAL RICHELIEU. There is that.

MILADY. How long do I have?

CARDINAL RICHELIEU. A week at most.

MILADY. And how do I get to him?

CARDINAL RICHELIEU. Document one: This gains you a private audience with the king. It says you're part of an embassy from Spain. You can wear a wig and lisp.

Document two: Safe passage out of the country. It will take you to Venice. I thought you'd enjoy Venice. Please say hello to the Borgias for me.

Document three, the most important of all: A pardon – in case you get caught. It's called a carte blanche. It has the force of law and is unbreakable, even by royal fiat.

MILADY. "It is by my order and for the benefit of the State that the bearer of this note has done what he has done." Signed by you.

CARDINAL RICHELIEU. It covers everything. I suggest you guard it with your life.

MILADY. I will also need to be paid a very great deal of money.

CARDINAL RICHELIEU. Oh, please, don't even think of bargaining with me. The sum of ten thousand crowns royal will be waiting for you in Venice. And don't say "what if it isn't" because if it wasn't there, you'd come back here and slit my throat.

MILADY. How touching. You're getting to know me. But one more thing. I intend to eliminate D'Artagnan and his lady love before I leave the country.

CARDINAL RICHELIEU. A matter of honor?

MILADY. I have no honor left. And I don't like losing.

CARDINAL RICHELIEU. Well you're out of luck. The queen has moved Miss Bonacieux for safekeeping.

MILADY. Where?

CARDINAL RICHELIEU. Sorry.

MILADY. I'll give you anything.

CARDINAL RICHELIEU. Anything?

MILADY. Any...thing.

CARDINAL RICHELIEU. Well. In that case. She's at the Carmelite Convent at Bethune.

MILADY. Excellent.

> *(She starts to leave.)*

CARDINAL RICHELIEU. Ah ah ah. I believe we have a bargain.

> *(She stands stock-still. He touches her cheek. Her shoulder...)*

MILADY. What do you want?

CARDINAL RICHELIEU. ...Nothing. I just wanted to hear you ask.

> *(He goes to the door.)*

Perhaps I'll see you in Venice someday. Just don't play cards with the Borgias. They cheat.

(He exits. MILADY gathers her documents and puts them away. She takes a breath and opens the door to leave – and there, standing in the doorway, is ATHOS. His face is in shadow.)

MILADY. Who are you?

(He walks out of the shadow, backing her into the room.)

I said who are –

(She gasps.)

ATHOS. Your husband once upon a time.

MILADY. The Comte de la Fere. But I thought you were...

ATHOS. My name is Athos now. Just as yours is de Winter. Only I'm still the man I was, and you've become a fiend put on this earth to torture anyone who gets in your way.

MILADY. You made me what I am!

ATHOS. I made you nothing. I made you *nothing*! I loved you once. I would have moved the earth for you.

MILADY. And I loved you. And I still love you.

(As she goes to embrace him – snap! – the concealed dagger is in her hand and she tries to stab him, but he catches her wrist and disarms her, pushing her violently to the floor.)

I hate you! I was young and I could have changed! I got down on my knees and begged you for mercy! But you strung me up and left me for dead!

ATHOS. Hand me the documents.

MILADY. No!

(He pulls out a pistol and holds it to her head.)

ATHOS. Hand me the documents or I blow your brains out.

(She hesitates.)

ATHOS. You know I'll do it! Just give me an excuse! Go on! MAKE A MOVE!

MILADY. There! Take them!

> (**ATHOS** *takes the documents. As he stuffs them into his vest,* **MILADY** *makes her move. She springs up and retrieves her dagger. They struggle over it, but she's able to stab him.*)
>
> (**ATHOS** *cries out, holds his shoulder, and staggers backward to the ground. She tries to retrieve the documents but hears noises outside the door:*)

PORTHOS. *(Offstage.)* Athos!

ARAMIS. *(Offstage.)* Athos, are you all right?!

> (**MILADY** *cries out in frustration. She can't get to the documents in time and she flees the room.* **PORTHOS** *and* **ARAMIS** *run in.*)

PORTHOS. Athos! My dear fellow!

ARAMIS. What happened for heaven's sake?!

ATHOS. *Ahh!*

> *(The wound.)*

We must to the king. Quickly.

ARAMIS. The king?

ATHOS. There's going to be an attempt on his life. And you must find D'Artagnan. Milady knows where Constance is! Quickly! Quickly!

> *(Instantly we hear the bells of a convent and we go to:)*

Scene Eight

(The Carmelite Convent at Bethune. We're in a chapel. The **ABBESS**, *a wonderful old gossip, is in the room as* **CONSTANCE** *enters, carrying flowers.)*

CONSTANCE. Oh Reverend Mother look at these! I've just picked them from the garden.

ABBESS. Aren't they beautiful. I think you're getting used to our ways.

CONSTANCE. I'm trying, Mother. Oh, and wait. The gardener says we have a visitor at the gate. He says she's from Paris and needs shelter for the night.

ABBESS. I'll see to it right away. Why don't you bring some refreshments in.

CONSTANCE. Of course.

*(***CONSTANCE*** exits in one direction and the* **ABBESS** *goes to the other door. When she opens it,* **MILADY** *is there.)*

ABBESS. Oh. Hello. You must be the visitor.

MILADY. Forgive me for intruding Mother, but I find myself an orphan in the storm. May I stay with you for a night or two? I won't be here long, I assure you.

ABBESS. Yes of course you may. And you are –?

MILADY. The Countess de Winter.

ABBESS. Oh, well! And I understand that you come from Paris. Were you there during the attack on the king?

MILADY. Word travels quickly.

THE ABBESS. Oh my dear, we know all about it. Thank the Lord God Jesus Christ he survived.

MILADY. Yes, aren't we lucky.

ABBESS. They say the assassin was a woman. Did you know that? I was told they had her under arrest for a moment but she slipped through their fingers and got away.

MILADY. So I heard.

ABBESS. She must be remarkably evil, that's all I can say.

MILADY. Or perhaps her life has been very difficult.

ABBESS. They're bound to find her.

MILADY. Why do you say that?

ABBESS. The entire country is looking for her! And can you imagine what they'll do to her when they catch her? I almost feel sorry for the poor thing.

MILADY. Oh, I'm sure she has no use for your pity.

CONSTANCE. Hello.

> (**CONSTANCE** *has appeared at the door with a tray bearing a bottle of brandy and three glasses.*)

ABBESS. Constance. Come in. The Countess de Winter. Constance Bonacieux.

CONSTANCE. How do you do? Cook is asking for you. She needs advice.

ABBESS. Of course she does. You two get acquainted. I'll be right back.

> (*She exits.*)

MILADY. I've seen you at court.

CONSTANCE. I'm sorry. I-I don't remember you.

MILADY. Oh, I was never as important as a lady-in-waiting. I was decoration. Do you miss it terribly?

CONSTANCE. I miss my friends. And my – ...

MILADY. Your lover?

CONSTANCE. My best friend.

MILADY. Monsieur D'Artagnan.

CONSTANCE. You know D'Artagnan?!

MILADY. Extremely well. We grew up together.

CONSTANCE. He's never mentioned you.

MILADY. This was some time back, in Gascony.

CONSTANCE. Gascony? He talks about it all the time! Oh this is wonderful! Can I tell you a secret?

MILADY. (*Stroking her hair.*) Oh please do.

CONSTANCE. I'm in hiding from the cardinal, but D'Artagnan is coming to take me away.

MILADY. Well of course he is. We must all have hope.

CONSTANCE. No, I mean today! We're going to be married! I received this letter this morning. It's from him!

*(She pulls out a letter. **MILADY** goes pale.)*

He's coming here with his friend Athos and the others. Do you see?

MILADY. Does he say when he expects to arrive?

CONSTANCE. *Today. This morning!* Isn't that... *Wait!* Listen! I hear horses!

(She springs to the window.)

MILADY. *No, stop!* Let *me* look! It could be the cardinal's guards. You said they're after you.

CONSTANCE. But I could just –

MILADY. *Stay back!* ...My darling girl, if they caught even a glimpse of you, you'd be in danger.

*(**MILADY** looks out the window and sees **D'ARTAGNAN**, **SABINE**, and the **THREE MUSKETEERS**, who have just dismounted. We see them also.)*

Oh my God! It's the cardinal himself!

CONSTANCE. Oh, no!

*(**CONSTANCE** sits down with fear.)*

MILADY. *(Speaking fast, her wits buzzing.)* Listen to me, we have to act quickly. You must come with me. My carriage is at the back of the convent.

*(She hurries to the door, but **CONSTANCE** hasn't moved.)*

Would you come on!

CONSTANCE. I can't move. I-I'm too frightened.

MILADY. You *must* move! Right now! Quickly!

CONSTANCE. *I can't!* Just...just save yourself. I'll be all right. I... I...

(**CONSTANCE** *is rooted to the chair, unable to breathe, much less move.* **MILADY** *makes a quick decision.*)

MILADY. All right, now listen. Do as I say. Close your eyes. *Close them*. Good. Now take deep breaths...

(*As* **MILADY** *talks she pours some wine from the pitcher into a goblet. Then she opens the top of a ring on one of her fingers and pours the contents of the ring into the wine. It's a powder that changes the color of the wine; and alas, it's poisonous.*)

Good. That's very good. Just try to relax. Everything is going to work out beautifully, I promise...

CONSTANCE. I'm so frightened!

MILADY. Shhh. There. Now open your eyes and drink this down.

CONSTANCE. What?

MILADY. It will calm your nerves, I promise.

CONSTANCE. But I-I don't really want to –

MILADY. *Drink it*. You have to trust me. All of this will soon be a dream.

(**CONSTANCE** *hesitates for a moment...then she drinks the poison. Every drop. All the way down. At this precise moment we hear a loud knocking at the door.*)

D'ARTAGNAN. *(Offstage.)* Constance?! Constance, can you hear me?!

CONSTANCE. That's D'Artagnan's voice.

D'ARTAGNAN. *Constance?!*

CONSTANCE. *D'Artagnan!*

MILADY. *Shut up!*

CONSTANCE. But why did you lie to me –?

MILADY. Oh Christ and the Devil. You stupid fool.

CONSTANCE. Oh my God, *who are you*?!

(As **CONSTANCE** *looks at the goblet in dismay,* **MILADY** *pulls out her dagger and holds it at* **CONSTANCE**'s *throat.)*

MILADY. One sound and I kill you both. Do you understand?

*(***CONSTANCE*** nods, and* **MILADY** *pulls her into the shadows. At this moment* **D'ARTAGNAN**, **SABINE**, *and the* **MUSKETEERS** *burst into the room.)*

D'ARTAGNAN. I heard her voice!

ARAMIS. This way!

PORTHOS. Quickly!

ATHOS. I'll try around back!

SABINE. I'll try the stable!

(They all rush out. As soon as they're gone, **MILADY** *drags* **CONSTANCE** *back to the center and thrusts her to the floor.)*

CONSTANCE. I don't understand! What do you want with me?! *D'Artagnan! Help! I – ahhhh! The wine!*

(The poison is working and **CONSTANCE** *drops to her knees. Instantly,* **MILADY** *pulls out the rosary beads. She whips them around* **CONSTANCE**'s *neck and pulls ruthlessly.)*

MILADY. You should have had better taste in men.

*(***CONSTANCE*** falls to the floor, at which point* **MILADY** *rushes to the door and opens it to leave –)*

(But there in the doorway is **SABINE** *with a sword. She punches* **MILADY** *with all her might and sends her reeling across the room with a cry.)*

(And now **SABINE** *attacks, remembering everything her father taught her. The duel is ferocious and terrifying. They use swords, knives, and even the rosary beads. In the end* **SABINE** *is almost killed, but she pulls the trick*

she learned from her father at the beginning of the play:)

SABINE. Hey! Snap! Ha!

(And she thrusts her sword into **MILADY***'s chest.)*

MILADY. *Ahh!*

SABINE. That's for trying to kill my brother.

(She stabs her again.)

And that's for trying to kill me.

(With a gasp of knowledge, **MILADY** *dies. At which moment the* **MUSKETEERS** *and* **D'ARTAGNAN** *run in.)*

CONSTANCE. D'Artagnan...

D'ARTAGNAN. Constance!

*(***D'ARTAGNAN*** rushes to* **CONSTANCE** *and cradles her head in his arms.)*

CONSTANCE. You came for me...

D'ARTAGNAN. Of course I did.

CONSTANCE. *(The pain of the wound.) Ah!*

D'ARTAGNAN. Oh, Constance. Please don't go. Please stay with me. There's so much I want to say to you. I want to show you Gascony, where I was a little boy, and it will make you laugh, I promise. And you'll meet my father and mother, and Sabine will make you such a wonderful...

(He can't go on.)

CONSTANCE. Do you always talk so much? Always remember...how much I loved you.

(She dies.)

D'ARTAGNAN. Nooooo!

ATHOS. It shouldn't have ended like this. Not for any of us.

D'ARTAGNAN. *(Seething with anger.)* ...He'll pay for this. Do you hear me? The cardinal will pay. *As God is my witness!!*

(**D'ARTAGNAN** *springs up and runs out of the room.*)

SABINE. D'Artagnan, wait!

PORTHOS. Come back!

ARAMIS. Don't be a fool!

(**D'ARTAGNAN** *is gone.* **SABINE**, **ARAMIS**, *and* **PORTHOS** *run after him.* **ATHOS** *remains, staring at* **CONSTANCE**, *then at* **MILADY**, *and he cannot speak.*)

Scene Nine

(The royal garden. The **KING**, *still bandaged from the assassination attempt, is just finishing a game of chess with* **CARDINAL RICHELIEU**. **TREVILLE**, **ROCHEFORT**, *and the* **QUEEN** *are there also.)*

KING LOUIS. Checkmate! Ha haaaa! Marvelous! Checkmate, checkmate, checkmate!

*(**D'ARTAGNAN** rushes in.)*

Hello? What's this?

TREVILLE. D'Artagnan?

D'ARTAGNAN. Excuse me for interrupting, Your Highness, but I need to speak with Cardinal Richelieu.

CARDINAL RICHELIEU. What's the meaning of this? You little upstart. Can't you see that we're having an argghhhhh!

D'ARTAGNAN. I'LL KILL YOU! I SWORE TO KILL YOU AND I'LL KILL YOU NOW!!

*(**D'ARTAGNAN** is strangling the **CARDINAL**, just as the **CARDINAL** has strangled **ROCHEFORT** in the past. He's grabbed him 'round the neck with one hand and is virtually lifting him off the ground.)*

CARDINAL RICHELIEU. Rochefort! ROCHEFORT!!

ROCHEFORT. *(Pleased to see it.)* I'm not sure there's much I can do to help.

CARDINAL RICHELIEU. Arghhhh! Arghhhh!

*(**SABINE**, **ATHOS**, **PORTHOS**, *and* **ARAMIS** *rush in.)*

ARAMIS. Stop!

PORTHOS. You fool!

ATHOS. Don't do it!

SABINE. D'Artagnan, stop it! Please! You'll be hanged! ...D'Arty, stop!

*(**D'ARTAGNAN** drops the **CARDINAL**, who is gasping for air and shaking with rage.)*

CARDINAL RICHELIEU. How dare you?! ...*How dare you?!*

TREVILLE. Athos, what's going on?

CARDINAL RICHELIEU. *(Crazed with anger, pulling **ROCHEFORT**'s sword.) Arrest this man this instant! Send him to the block!*

KING LOUIS. Just wait, wait, wait. Athos?

ATHOS. Miss Bonacieux was murdered by the Countess de Winter. With the help of the cardinal.

QUEEN ANNE. Constance?

PORTHOS. Yes, Your Majesty.

QUEEN ANNE. Oh, no.

CARDINAL RICHELIEU. That's ridiculous. I had nothing to do with it.

D'ARTAGNAN. You sent her there! You knew where she was!

*(He leaps at the **CARDINAL** to strangle him again, but **ATHOS** grabs him and stops him.)*

CARDINAL RICHELIEU. Lies. Fabrications. I defy you to prove a word of it. And I want this man arrested instantly. Rochefort!

ROCHEFORT. *(Shrugs helplessly.)* You have my sword, Your Eminence.

CARDINAL RICHELIEU. Your Majesty, tell your guards to arrest him, I insist on it! You saw what he did. The law demands it. You know it does!

KING LOUIS. Yes, yes. Of course. He's right, I'm afraid. There's nothing I can do about it. The boy will hang.

SABINE. No!

CARDINAL RICHELIEU. Arrest him!

*(**D'ARTAGNAN** steps forward and stands tall.)*

D'ARTAGNAN. Let them hang me if they must. I have done what is right.

(**ARAMIS** *and* **PORTHOS** *reluctantly begin to lead* **D'ARTAGNAN** *away, but* **ATHOS** *speaks up.*)

ATHOS. Wait. D'Artagnan, this is yours now. Show it to the king.

(**ATHOS** *pulls out the pardon – the carte blanche – which he took from Milady. He hands it to* **D'ARTAGNAN**, *who hands it to the* **KING**.)

KING LOUIS. *(Reading.)* "It is by my order and for the benefit of the State that the bearer of this note has done what he has done." Signed Cardinal Richelieu. Oh. Well. Then he's off the hook.

CARDINAL RICHELIEU. Let me see that! I take it back!

KING LOUIS. I'm afraid you can't. It's a carte blanche. That's the law, you know, and you do love the law.

(*The* **CARDINAL** *is enraged; then draws himself up.*)

CARDINAL RICHELIEU. *(To* **D'ARTAGNAN**.) I strongly suggest that you watch your back.

(*He heads for the exit and as he does, everyone else turns his or her back to him. He walks silently past them, fuming with rage.*)

Rochefort! Now! You imbecile!

(**ROCHEFORT** *follows.*)

(*He smacks* **ROCHEFORT** *with a resounding thwack and they both leave.*)

D'ARTAGNAN. Forgive me for intruding, Your Majesty. I apologize.

KING LOUIS. Oh not at all. I've been wanting to do that to the cardinal for years.

TREVILLE. D'Artagnan. You're just like your father. Impetuous. Disorderly. And very brave. I'd say it's about time you were a musketeer.

PORTHOS. Well past time, if you ask me.

D'ARTAGNAN. Monsieur, I-I'm very honored.

TREVILLE. As well you should be.

D'ARTAGNAN. But I don't know if this is the time, in light of Constance. I-I mean...

>   *(He turns away with emotion.)*

SABINE. D'Arty. I think it is the time. And she would have been very proud of you.

>   *(**D'ARTAGNAN** hugs **SABINE**, then turns to **TREVILLE**.)*

D'ARTAGNAN. All right. Thank you, sir.

TREVILLE. Well kneel, kneel.

>   *(**ARAMIS** and **PORTHOS** go off and come back with a hat and a cape and a sword. Music plays.* The lights change. **ARAMIS** offers the cape to the **QUEEN**, who puts it around **D'ARTAGNAN**'s shoulders. **PORTHOS** places the hat on **D'ARTAGNAN**'s head, and **ATHOS** hands his sword to the **KING** for the purpose of the knighting.)*

>   *(As **TREVILLE** delivers the following speech, the light changes so that the tableau glows as though out of the greatest book we ever read in our childhood.)*

By the power invested in me as Captain of the Royal Musketeers to the King of France, the Duchy of Lorraine and the Territory of the High Belgian States, I hereby invest you with the rank of Musketeer and charge you with the defense of the realm and, in particular, the person of the king himself whosoe'er he be. And I charge you to acquit these duties and yourself

---

*A license to produce *The Three Musketeers* does not include a performance license for any third-party or copyrighted music. Licensees should create an original composition or use music in the public domain. For further information, please see Music Use Note on page 3.

to the highest degree with courage, with humility, and with honor. In the name of all that is holy and good,

ALL. Amen.

> (**ATHOS** *turns and speaks to the audience, as then does everyone in the cast, in turn.*)

ATHOS. Life is fragile.

PORTHOS. Life is a banquet.

ARAMIS. Life can play tricks on you.

ATHOS. The three musketeers,

D'ARTAGNAN. And D'Artagnan,

SABINE. And Sabine.

PORTHOS. Buried Constance Bonacieux at the Carmelite Convent at Bethune with all the appropriate rites and duties of the Catholic Church.

QUEEN ANNE. Queen Anne returned to her husband.

KING LOUIS. King Louis the Thirteenth fathered Louis the Fourteenth;

BUCKINGHAM. Queen Anne never saw Buckingham again.

TREVILLE. Treville went on training young musketeers.

CARDINAL RICHELIEU. And Cardinal Richelieu was banished to Italy where he lived out his life playing cards with the Borgias.

ATHOS. Life is fate.

QUEEN ANNE. Life is hope.

SABINE. Life is different than we ever imagined it.

D'ARTAGNAN. But most of all, life is an adventure.

> (*At this moment we hear a musket shot and a scream – the lights restore to normal – and suddenly a* **HAGGARD OLD WOMAN** *races on in desperation.*)

OLD WOMAN. Help! Help! Please help me!

PORTHOS. What's the matter?!

ARAMIS. What is it?!

OLD WOMAN. Oh please, good sirs! My daughter! She's been kidnapped! She works for a count who's visiting Paris and the count has enemies. Terrible enemies!

PORTHOS. Who are his enemies?!

OLD WOMAN. I have no idea! But he comes from a little island called Monte Cristo.

ATHOS. Gentlemen?

ARAMIS. What are we waiting for?

ATHOS. Let's go.

PORTHOS. Wait! Aren't we forgetting something?

> *(He draws his sword – and then they all do.)*

FOUR MUSKETEERS. All for one!

> *(**SABINE** makes a move. She's dying to join them. **D'ARTAGNAN** sees it and he does what's right.)*

D'ARTAGNAN. Oh, go ahead.

SABINE. And one for all!

ALL FIVE. Chaaaaaaaaaaaaaaarge!

> *(Their swords raised, the five friends charge off to help those in distress.)*

End of Play